"I want you," Valentin said. "I want you, but I won't take you."

Adriana struggled to find her voice. "Who invited you?"

"You did." He glared at her with those strange golden eyes, then turned his back and walked away.

Angry, dazed, feeling as if she'd been seduced against her will, then thrown aside—and all without him so much as making a move toward her—Adriana watched him disappear into the deep shadows of the buildings.

Then her pride took over, and she turned to walk toward home. She told herself she'd felt desire, a craving more fiery and fierce than she'd ever experienced in her life, but she could have resisted him if she'd wanted to.

Would she ever see him again? She wished she didn't care. He was mysterious, strange, sexy, arrogant...and definitely more dangerous than any man she'd ever met in her life.

Dear Reader,

We have another thrilling, chilling treat in store for you this month. Jeanne Rose is back with another compelling look at the dark side of love.

Good Night, My Love is the story of Adriana Thorn, who falls for mysterious nightwalker Valentin Kadar, only to wonder whether he is friend—and lover—or foe. You, too, will fall in love with the enigmatic Valentin as Adriana seeks the answer to her question.

Next month, look for Kimberly Raye's second book, *Now and Forever.* And the month after that, join Evelyn Vaughn as she completes her four-book miniseries, THE CIRCLE. As always, we hope you enjoy your walk on the dark side of love.

Yours,

Leslie Wainger
Senior Editor and Editorial Coordinator

Please address questions and book requests to:
Silhouette Reader Service
U.S.: 3010 Walden Ave., P.O. Box 1325, Buffalo, NY 14269
Canadian: P.O. Box 609, Fort Erie, Ont. L2A 5X3

JEANNE ROSE

Published by Silhouette Books
America's Publisher of Contemporary Romance

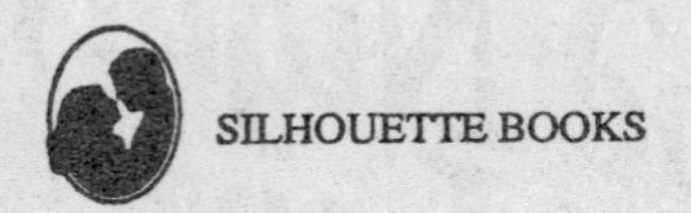

ISBN 0-373-27064-X

GOOD NIGHT, MY LOVE

This edition published by arrangement with Harlequin Books S.A.

Printed in U.S.A.

Books by Jeanne Rose

Silhouette Shadows

The Prince of Air and Darkness #26
Heart of Dreams #55
Good Night, My Love #84

Silhouette Romance

Believing in Angels #913
Love on the Run #1027

JEANNE ROSE

is the newest pseudonym of Patricia Pinianski and Linda Sweeney. The Chicagoans have been a team since 1982, when they met in a writing class. Now Linda teaches writing at two suburban community colleges and works for *Writer's Digest*, while Patricia makes writing her full-time focus. Patricia and Linda are happy they can combine their fascination with the mysterious and magical with their belief in the triumph of love. Patricia and Linda are also known as Lynn Patrick, and Patricia writes as Patricia Rosemoor.

For Linda's nieces and nephew,
who enjoy scary books and movies

PROLOGUE

"Night, the eternal, the elemental, owns the earth. Night wraps reality with dreams and great, starry wings.

"The sun rises and the sun sets, but its fire burns far away. The sun merely visits.

"After dark, the city flares like a tiny flame in the all-encompassing blackness. Closer, the blaze splinters into a multitude of lights, an electric net that stretches for miles upon miles.

"But nothing catches the night.

"Night breathes. Night beats like a heart.

"Hear the throb of traffic, the rumble of the subway deep beneath the ground.

"Night needs. Night demands.

"Feel your pulse quicken, your breath rise and fall.

"Night lives.

"Night wears another face...sometimes dangerous, often thrilling, always timeless in its beauty.

"If you know this, you know me.

"Meet me after dark...."

The radio broadcast segued into music, an old Doors number that started slow, then rose in tempo and volume, finally obliterating the soft, sensuous female voice. Though the woman had already imprinted herself on his soul.

He knew her.

Adriana Thorn was the deejay at After Dark, a popular dance club located in downtown Chicago. He'd tuned in for the first time last week, inadvertently catching a midnight show transmitted from that establishment.

Adriana called herself the "Daughter of the Night," and gave poetic monologues so riveting, she'd doubtlessly put the club on the city entertainment map. No wonder a radio station had decided to send her lush voice zinging along the airwaves for an hour every Saturday night.

He sat back in his chair, allowing himself to conjure Adriana in his imagination. He felt certain she possessed large smoky eyes, rich dark hair, full lips...and, of course, a long, graceful throat. She'd be intelligent, as well as naturally, beautifully sensual. Her pale skin would smell like hothouse blooms and be as velvety smooth to the touch. Her taste... He stopped at that. No use torturing himself.

And with a bitter smile, he rose to pace about the huge, empty, darkened room. No lamps, no flames, in the great maw of a fireplace, not even a candle. He didn't need them.

The dim glow of the streetlights through cracked, latticed windowpanes produced more than enough illumination.

As usual, restless in the deep night hours, he decided to go out for a walk. Approaching the fireplace mantel, he switched the radio off and picked up his dark glasses.

Outside, on the porch of the decaying Victorian mansion, he carefully locked the door behind him. Not that anyone would try to break in, not after the way he'd handled the last would-be thief.

The old floorboards should squeak beneath his feet. But they didn't. His step was light.

He left and headed down the sidewalk, which seemed surprisingly deserted, especially for the seedy center of Uptown on a warm spring night. Only a drunk staggered out of his way as he glided onward, passing apartment buildings with doorways that smelled of urine and lower windows that were boarded up.

The business district started at the end of the block, and he put on the dark glasses to protect his sensitive eyes from the neon glare. Several men argued outside a bar, while a woman wearing tight shorts and long earrings tried to flag down a car. Bang Me, Baby sparkled in sequins across her rear.

As he stared at the hooker, she paused for a moment, turning to see what or who had attracted her attention. But she didn't really notice him, merely sensed his subtle, fleeting presence. As did the men, who suddenly decided to take their argument elsewhere.

Again the sardonic smile. They needn't worry. He hadn't been dangerous for years...at least, not most of the time.

And he never drew attention to himself unless he wanted it.

Tonight he craved nothing from the scrabble of people who drove up and down these streets or called to each other from open windows and doors.

Night wears another face.

Well, this one was painted . . . with cheap makeup.

He longed for more elegant darkness.

A few blocks farther, his acute hearing picked up the soft lapping call of the lake. Passing a bank whose clock showed it to be nearly 1:00 a.m., he crossed a street, traversed an underpass and finally stood on the sandy beach. Waves swept in, along with a light, swirling fog.

Above, a white moon slid behind a bank of charcoal clouds. Downtown Chicago beckoned, a curve of glittering radiance across the black water.

He savored the beauty.

If you know this, you know me.

The wind gusted and plucked at the edges of his jacket, fluttering the material like wings.

He thought of her, her lush voice, her obvious passion for the element in which he loved and lived.

Meet me after dark.

Cynicism fought desire and lost.

He would accept the invitation.

CHAPTER ONE

At one in the morning, Adriana Thorn took off her headphones and pushed her chair back with a relieved sigh. The radio broadcast was over. She'd had experience with the medium some years before, having worked as a deejay at an obscure AM station in the suburbs, yet sending her voice out into the stratosphere always made her feel a bit disoriented.

She preferred a more tangible audience like that of After Dark. The glass walls of the club's sound booth separated her and the crowd outside, but she could gauge their reactions to her monologues and mixes, could feel she was interacting with them. A nonconformist who'd never quite fit in with her family, a night person continually at odds with the world's daytime schedule, she appreciated company in the dark hours.

Making sure the stack of CDs was ready for her next set, she left the booth, locking it behind her. On Saturdays, a live band played for the next hour or so. Tonight, the rock group that had been scheduled was running late, still setting up.

A skinny guitarist strutted past, his shirt open to the waist, his hair long. He tossed wild strands back from his face and gave Adriana the eye. "Hi ya, babe. Catch you for a drink later?"

She smiled. "We'll see."

Which was probably enough to discourage such a pretty young man. She'd outgrown his type—the kind who thought the earth and its female population revolved around him.

Though, she was still attracted to men who did most of their living at night. She'd dated her share of musicians and actors. Once she'd even gotten involved with a cop. World weary and street smart, he'd exuded an aura of danger that had fascinated her.

Danger.

She had to be careful. Her last romance with a free-spirited performance artist had left her broke and a little afraid, both reasons for her moving in with her older sister, Jennifer.

She observed the crowd as she skirted the dance floor. Beneath soaring Gothic-style eaves, the usual Saturday night revelers boogied with their weekend dates. Laughter rippled around her and smiles sparkled in the dim light. There would be requests later, selections easy enough to come up with. Adriana wouldn't be experimenting with anything unusual like she did on weeknights—mixes of different types of music blended with special effects like owl hoots and wolf howls. Not that she still possessed all the records and tapes and CDs she'd once had since her collection had been stolen.

Frank Nieman, the club's manager, waved and pushed his way through the throng to slide an arm about her shoulders. "Great work." A nervous man with a slight accent, he wore black wire-rimmed glasses and a gray-streaked ponytail. "I don't know where you get your ideas, but that monologue was phenomenal."

"Sometimes I read poetry before I go to sleep." Reading at night was a hobby she'd pursued since childhood when her parents had made her go to bed too early and she'd sneaked a flashlight under the covers. "Don't expect the same caliber of material at two. I save the best for the broadcast."

"Leave modesty to those without your brilliance."

Adriana returned Frank's grin. It was nice to be appreciated. Furthermore, she considered the manager a friend, though she sometimes thought he'd like to be more. When he took his leave, she strolled toward the massive doors opening into the lounge area of After Dark. The smaller space was situated near the entrance of the building that had once been an auditorium.

A long, curving bar in the shape of a quarter moon dominated one end of the room, while the adjoining area featured candlelit booths and a gypsy fortune-teller whose dark red curls were wrapped with a bright scarf. Noting that her pal, Irina Murphy, was busy reading tarot cards for a couple of customers, Adriana sauntered over to the bar.

"Tonic water and lime, please, Peter," she told the bartender.

"Nothing stronger?"

"Since when do I drink on the job?" Actually, she rarely drank at all, except for an occasional glass of wine at dinner.

"C'mon, let loose. Get wild and crazy for once."

He was teasing, so she joked back. "I'm plenty wild and crazy already." At least, according to her sister.

She moved away, again glancing toward the tarot readings. Irina remained busy, her gaminelike face serious. Adriana decided she should try a reading herself some night. Half Irish and half Romanian Gypsy, Irina claimed to have inherited psychic abilities from two different cultures.

Adriana glanced at her watch, surprised to see it was only ten past one. She had plenty of time until her next set and should probably be wandering around. Frank said her presence added ambience, which is why she always dressed in floaty dark clothing and celestial jewelry.

Tonight she wore a long midnight blue chiffon skirt strewn with stars and a matching jacket over a wine red satin bustier. More stars, clusters of rhinestones, dangled from her ears.

A draft from the door behind her made those earrings swing, her skirt flutter... while at the same time raising prickles on the back of her neck. She had the distinct, sudden feeling that someone was staring hard at her.

She turned, her gaze meeting that of a tall, lean, somber man who stood alone in the doorway.

That is, their gazes would meet if he weren't wearing dark glasses.

A bit pretentious, she thought, while at the same time finding herself intrigued. Probably in his mid-thirties, at least a dozen years older than the rock guitarist, the stranger had high cheekbones, a straight nose and a wide, sensual mouth. His thick black hair was long, if stylishly cut. His dark clothing appeared fashionable yet understated. And there was something exotic, foreign looking, about him....

"Adriana Thorn."

He approached directly, startling her. His voice was deep, melodic, tinged with a light accent. She always noted tones and timbres, her profession based on sound.

"Have we met?" she asked. Though she didn't think so. Surely she would remember a man who topped her by several inches, though she was quite tall and wearing heels. She would also remember a man with such proud bearing and unusual looks.

"I am sorry to say we have not met...until now. I am what you would call a fan."

Adriana had met many fans before, sometimes very weird ones. "How nice," she said cautiously, fascinated despite herself.

"I came to express my admiration for you," he went on, then smiled. "But you must pardon me. I have forgotten to introduce myself." He offered his hand. "Valentin Kadar."

Definitely foreign. Wondering about his origins, Adriana placed her hand in his, not expecting him to raise it to his lips in a graceful gesture. His kiss was cool and dry—though the electric shiver that ran up and down her spine, then shot out to other parts, felt anything but cool. Goose bumps rose on her arms. Uncomfortable, she wished the man would let go.

He did so, smiling wider and with a flash of strong white teeth. "Let us sit down for a moment, shall we? I'll buy you another drink."

She was about to point out that all the booths were occupied when a couple rose right in front of them, hurrying off with cocktails in hand.

She found herself sliding into a seat. "I'm only having tonic and lime."

Sitting opposite her, he gestured for a waitress, a new employee Adriana didn't know very well. The woman quickly appeared.

"Tonic and lime, and a cognac," Val stated.

When the waitress hurried away, Adriana asked, "Did you say your name is Valentin?"

"You may call me Val."

The way he spoke, the easy authority with which he'd handled the waitress, made her think he was used to wielding power. He obviously had bucks—the black suit jacket he wore over an equally elegant dark shirt reeked of Armani. Not that she required a man to have money.

Startled, Adriana realized she was considering Valentin Kadar as something more than a professional admirer. But then, why wouldn't she contemplate a little romance, not having gotten such a jolt from anyone since Stone Drake, the performance artist who'd run out on her. Literally.

Thinking about Stone, however—the brooding intensity that had initially attracted her—rang a warning bell.

"Do you come here often?" she asked.

"I have never been here before."

She frowned. "You said you were a fan."

"From the radio."

Then how had he known who she was, what she looked like? The club hadn't released a publicity photo and there had been no newspaper articles.

But before she could question him, he told her, "I recognized you the moment I saw you. I was certain you were as beautiful as your words. And you are. Such perfect skin, such lovely eyes." He leaned forward, mesmerizing her with his attention. "Gray, aren't they? And your hair shimmers like a fall of silk."

Very poetic. And very forward, she thought when he reached across the table to brush a long strand from her cheek. His finger took its time, leaving a trail of warmth across her skin.

Her goose bumps got goose bumps.

"You hold yourself like a queen," Val Kadar went on, giving her space again, leaning back in his chair. "You live up to your title—Daughter of the Night."

Her face warmed. "Well, I took some acting lessons in college." Plus she wore dramatic makeup and a burgundy rinse in her dark brown hair for work. "In a way, I'm playing a part."

Even if it fit her fantasies.

"One cannot *act* lovely. Real beauty must come from within."

She dropped her eyes, feeling a bit shy, unusual for her. She handled most people with practiced aplomb, including men. But most people blathered. He seemed quite centered and serious, perfectly sure of himself.

So she changed the focus to him. "You're European, aren't you, Mr. Kadar?"

He nodded, though he offered no further information. Again, he urged, "Please, call me Val."

"Oh, right... Val."

Still seeking to feel comfortable, she searched for eyes behind the dark glasses. The opaque lenses only reflected flickering candlelight and made his skin seem pale. "I don't mean to get personal... but do you have some problem with your eyes? Or are you merely trying to appear mysterious?"

"I would never try to appear as anything but what I am."

And he took the glasses off. He was even more striking without them, his eyes a golden shade of brown that seemed to glow through the dark.

A thrill shot through her when he fastened that gaze on her, intensely drinking in the sight of her. Without the glasses, his persona became even more powerful. Heat spread from her middle. An attraction like this was definitely dangerous for a woman who'd barely gotten over a bad relationship. She glanced around, pretending to be interested in the people around them as the waitress delivered their order. Then she concentrated on stirring the swizzle stick.

"So what do you do, Val?" she asked.

"Do?" He sipped at his cognac.

"You have a profession, right? I trust I'm not prying." Not unless what he did was either illegal and-or immoral....

"You are asking about work?"

He paused for a moment, as if thinking of a good answer, which didn't add to her confidence about his character. Forget about fearing intense, instant attraction. To be interested in someone involved in questionable activities—yet another night type—would be truly dangerous.

Then he said, "At the moment, I dabble with photography," and she let go a big breath.

Dabbling? Perhaps he was independently wealthy. "What kind of photography?"

"Night visions." He leaned forward, though this time he kept his hands to himself. "But I came here to see you. I don't want to talk about my own boring life. How did you come to have such a love affair with the dark?"

The way he lingered over the words *love affair* made her believe he knew just how much he attracted her. Again, she dared to meet his eyes, part of her wanting to lose herself in their golden depths, while yet another part wanting to run away. How strange.

She admitted, "I'm a night person, always have been. I don't know why. I'm never fully awake until late afternoon. My body clock just works that way."

"I can understand that."

His hungry glance slid over her. She was aware that the tops of her breasts were visible, pushed up by the bustier. Again, warmth crept through her when his gaze lingered there.

That's why she was surprised when he asked, "Do you like your profession?"

"Very much. I like to entertain people." And having some renown, even though she felt on display at times and vulnerable when her voice seemed to establish intimacies with strangers.

He chatted on, fielding more questions, until she was talking about her background before coming to After Dark. Off-guard, she found herself not only discussing her work, but also the places she'd lived before, her goals for the future, even the titles of some of her favorite books.

She almost forgot to balk when Val got too personal.

"Have you ever been in love?"

"Well . . . sure." At least, she'd fancied herself head over heels for Stone.

"You hesitate. I do not think this man was your true soul mate."

"If there is such a thing."

"Oh, there is, believe me," he said, his voice warm and seductive. Though she noted his smile didn't reach his eyes.

Another warning bell sounded. She couldn't help a wisecrack. "What's coming next? A proposition?"

"Is that what you want?"

She'd expected to put him on the spot and he'd turned it around. "Of course not." Despite her attraction. "I hardly know you."

He laughed for the first time since they'd met, a soft sound that made strange chills run up and down her spine. "Perhaps you do not know me, but I know you."

How arrogant. Even if his saying it sounded sexy as all get-out. "Inspired by my monologue?"

"I listened closely."

As attentively as he'd listened to all the details he'd managed to drag out of her just now, no doubt. When she'd said she hardly knew him, she'd exaggerated. All Valentin Kadar had told her about himself was that he was European and that he dabbled in photography. The warning bells became louder, pealing from the depths of her intuition. Somehow, she knew she must avoid letting this mystery man have the upper hand.

"You may think you know me. But radio monologues and bar conversation can't tell you everything about a person's life."

"Though much can be revealed, lying just beneath the surface." He mused, "I know what it is like to watch the night pass by, while everyone else is sleeping. Beautiful but often lonely...."

He spoke quite seriously. This was no glib line. Yet she felt relieved when she caught sight of Frank gesturing at her, indicating the next set was coming up. An hour had passed? Disconcerted because she'd forgotten the time, she rose in a flurry.

"Excuse me, I have to go."

"We can continue this conversation later," said Val.

Though she should rush off, she paused. He couldn't assume things. "I won't be seeing you afterward. I'm heading home." When he remained enigmatically silent, she added, "I don't go out with anyone unless we've gotten to know each other." And, as Jennifer had suggested, daylight was safer. "Unless we've had lunch—"

Val's eyebrows winged up, and he said, "I don't do lunch," although he was looking at her as if she were a tasty morsel.

Her eyes widened.

"Adriana!" shouted Frank.

She started and spun away, only glancing back over her shoulder as she breezed through the door. But Valentin Kadar had disappeared, his cognac left sitting on the table.

If it weren't for that glass, she could almost believe she'd imagined the entire exchange.

Adriana still remembered every detail of her conversation an hour or so later. She'd brooded about Val all through the set and wondered if she'd turned off a truly fascinating man because of the distrust she'd built up over Stone. She had no idea as to why Valentin Kadar didn't *do* lunch, but she could have given him an alternative, asked him if he'd like to accompany her on an outing with some other people.

She tried not to look too eager as she returned to the bar. Disappointingly enough, Val wasn't among the customers being approached for last call. But Irina and Peter were making plans to go out for a very late supper.

Irina urged, "Come on, Adriana. We're going to that Mexican place on Broadway. You like their cheese quesadillas."

"I'm not hungry." In case she'd missed something, she peered into the room's shadows.

"You could keep us company for an hour or two, have a little chat."

An hour or two? The mention of passing time reminded Adriana of her plans with her sister.

A stockbroker, sunny Jennifer Thorn rose at dawn and went to sleep with the birds. But she cared about Adriana and had always tried to understand her. She'd said she wanted to go out for brunch and a long drive the next day so they could catch up on things.

Adriana intended to keep that date. She owed her sister. And if she was going to be in the least bit coherent in the morning, she'd need to head straight home. She checked her watch.

"Good Lord, it's already after four." And she had to be up by nine at the latest. "I have to go home."

Irina's dark eyes twinkled as she quipped, "Hate to tell you this, Adriana, but there's no big hurry. You turned into a strange pumpkin a long time ago."

Adriana laughed. "Seriously, I have to go. How about if I call you tomorrow? I'd love to tell you about this man I met tonight."

"Someone on the dance floor?"

"In the bar." She pointed at a booth. "We were sitting right there, for at least an hour. You must have seen us."

Irina appeared puzzled. "Uh-uh. But then I had a real busy night."

Promising they'd talk—something Irina was quite good at, her unselfconscious chattering being one of her most charming qualities—Adriana took her leave, gathered up her wrap and left with a cluster of customers. A couple flagged down the lone taxi on which she'd set her sights.

"Damn."

But she could walk, her building being only a few blocks away. And the posh Gold Coast neighborhood bordering Michigan Avenue was busy at all hours on weekends, so it was relatively safe.

Besides, she enjoyed traveling the night.

A light wind teased her hair as she strode along. Amber streetlights floated against the city's mauve-dark sky. She waved to the tired driver of a horse-drawn carriage as he passed, returning to the stables. Since the weather was warming up, several street musicians had set up business in the little park near the city's historic Water Tower, a landmark left from the city's famous fire.

With a twinge, Adriana recognized the slim, shabby violinist playing a sad melody near one of the park benches. His open instrument case lay at his feet, though she worriedly noted he'd only collected some coins and a few small-denomination bills.

She tried to sound cheerful. "Eddie, how's it going?"

He glanced up, then grinned. "Hey, good to see you, Adriana. Tonight hasn't been bad."

Which meant he'd collected enough money to feed himself, if not pay for a room in a cheap hotel.

Adriana had known Eddie Szewicki for years, since college days when they'd run around together in the same small circle of friends. She'd worked with him, too, as an audio engineer on a couple of recordings he'd done with a now-defunct blues band. Eddie was a sad case, a mix of excellent classical training and frustrating flakiness. Not that orchestra seats were easy to obtain. But at least once upon a time he had used his musical talents to make a living playing with various local bands.

Unfortunately, Eddie hadn't been able to get a gig for at least a year, and Adriana feared that he was seriously depressed and becoming less and less able to take care of himself, even at the most basic level. She knew he had no siblings and that his elderly parents had passed on. She'd suggested counseling, had offered to get Eddie the help he so desperately needed to get his life back under control, had even suggested he sleep on her couch for a week or two while he looked for any job to keep him afloat. But he'd refused, put her off time and again.

So Adriana did the only thing she could.

Reaching into her purse, she pulled out a twenty and stuffed it into his hand. "Here's a penny for your melodies."

"Hey, that's way more'n a penny."

He tried to return the bill, but she refused. "It's only money." Besides, she made a good wage and had great sympathy for lost souls, and she and Eddie had once been close.

"If you don't care for the lady's money" came a smooth voice from behind her, "then perhaps you will take mine."

A hundred-dollar bill wafted into the violin case, causing the musician to widen his eyes. And Adriana nearly to jump out of her skin. Recognizing his voice if not his very presence, she whirled around to face Valentin Kadar.

"You followed me!" she accused, backing up.

Val's expression was inscrutable, his eyes hidden again by the dark glasses. "You should not walk from the club alone. You should be concerned for your safety."

She countered, "Yeah, safety from the likes of you."

"Definitely from the likes of me."

Maybe he really was some sort of criminal, she thought before insisting, "I don't have that far to go. And I know people around here."

"You are acquainted with some individuals. But not everyone on the street tonight is good-hearted, I can assure you."

Eddie was packing up his violin, eyeing the other man. "I'll walk you home, Adriana."

"That will not be necessary," said Val. When Eddie opened his mouth as if to object, Val removed his dark glasses, stared at him intently and gave him an imperious wave. "Go along."

Adriana couldn't believe the musician actually was obeying.

"Hold on a minute," she protested. "I can make my own decisions." She turned to Val. "Even a hundred-dollar donation doesn't give you the right to issue high-handed orders. I say Eddie's escorting me." But when she swung back to the musician, he was walking away. "Hey—"

"Leave him be," Val said. "He is tired, having slept on concrete for the past several nights. And someone tried to steal his instrument."

Wondering how in the world he'd come to that conclusion, Adriana was none too happy. Eyes darting, she noted several people strolling past, a police car stopped at the light on Michigan Avenue. She supposed she could scream up a storm if she wanted to.

"How do you know so much about Eddie?" she asked accusingly. "Did you give him the third degree, too?"

"Did I question him? No. On my way to the club, I passed by and overheard him telling his sad story to someone else."

She guessed that was possible, Eddie usually worked one spot an evening. "So why didn't you give him the hundred then?"

"I must admit your own generosity influenced me. You have a compassionate heart... as well as a strong spirit." He gestured toward the sidewalk that led through the little park. "Let me escort you, Adriana. I vow that you will be safe and you will be doing me a kindness. I, too, have suffered many difficult, lonely nights."

Lonely? She couldn't believe she felt a slight twinge for him. Was his admission that sincere? She glanced at his expression—grave, a little haunted... even with the penetrating gaze.

She made one last objection. "But you said I should be careful of the likes of you."

"You're a beautiful woman. You should be wary of any man."

Fast talking? Or had he really meant to warn her about men in general from the very first? But then, the danger she'd sensed from him all evening had hinged on her fear that she might once again become involved with the wrong man, not that she feared he was an attacker.

So she finally caved in, figuring there was no way she would allow herself to get close to anyone she had doubts about. "I suppose you could escort me partway."

After all, she really did have to get home and there *were* other people walking the streets, in case she needed help. Besides, Valentin Kadar continued to intrigue her with his mix of mystery and heady charm.

They crossed Michigan Avenue and turned north, walking past a hotel with a doorman standing guard under a canopy. There would also be a doorman at the entrance to her building, a grand old place that faced Oak Street Beach. Even if Val saw where she lived, he'd never be able to return on his own and breech the entrance without Jennifer or herself confirming the validity of his visit. She was safe.

She thought about the questions he'd asked her, about her own questions that had never been answered. "What part of Europe are you from?"

"A very old land . . . Hungary."

She sneaked a peek at him as he paced along beside her, his stride effortless. "And you're only visiting the U.S. to take photographs?"

"I have other business here, a matter that concerns my family."

"So you're not totally alone in the world."

"Technically, no."

What did that mean? "You don't get along with your relatives?"

"We have had our misunderstandings. I have taken a path that is different from theirs."

"I guess I can understand that. I make a good salary at After Dark. Hopefully, I even have a future there . . . or in some form of broadcasting. But my family disapproves of my job, my hours, my friends." And the unusual men she was attracted to, though she wasn't about to get into that. "They're more conservative than I am."

"We have many things in common. My family also follows the old ways."

They had stopped at the corner where Michigan Avenue ended and Lake Shore Drive began, a multilaned border that curved along the great lake and kept it from invading the city. Home was only a half a block away, but Adriana's eyes rested on the great, dark expanse of water on the other side of the drive. The wind picked up strength out here in the open and drove waves onto the beach, gray that paled to silver by streetlight. High rises stood about like silent sentinels, facing east, while older businesses and apartment buildings like her own faced north.

"We share a love of the night," Val went on, a low throb in his voice. "The dark speaks a different language."

His eyes were speaking some language she longed to understand. They were enticing...mesmerizing... drawing her closer to gaze into their very depths.

Swaying, Adriana fought the intense feeling that was overtaking her. She knew she should back off, race to the safety of her building, but she'd never felt so powerless...nor so drawn to explore the darkness in another human being. She didn't want to go anywhere but into Valentin Kadar's arms.

The thought made her light-headed, threw everything into soft focus, including the sounds of the restless lake.

Val must have sensed her sudden weakness, for, before she knew what was happening, she found herself locked tightly in his embrace. He splayed his fingers and ran them sensually through her hair.

"You are so beautiful, so extraordinary," he told her, and she felt his lips brush against hers. "Your mouth would be more intoxicating than the finest wine."

Aroused, nestled firmly against his hard chest—yet part of her removed from the embrace as if she were watching the action rather than participating—she said, "You have quite a way with words."

"I would rather have my way with you."

Her knees went weak as he kissed her, starting slow, probing with his tongue. Then he picked up the tempo, demanding more as he took hold of her hair and anchored her head with one hand. He was very strong. And his mouth was hungry...fierce. Wrapping her arms about him, she instinctively arched her back and let him take what he wanted.

Her mind floated and once more she had this feeling of detachment... and yet not.

Weird!

Val's kiss was a sensual demand as he moved his mouth from her lips to her throat, to the soft rise of her breasts and back again. Her breath left her. No man had ever excited her in quite this way before. Her heart pounded, her thighs quaked. Deep inside, she opened like a flower... and released her hold on reality.

There were only the two of them, the night, the water, the world spinning on its axis toward dawn.

Dawn.

A thin sliver of light appeared on the watery horizon.

With a sound that resembled a growl, he said, "I want you, but I won't take you."

Adriana started.

Her arms were wrapped around her middle. Val wasn't touching her. He *hadn't* touched her. She'd imagined the entire embrace. Even the kiss. Was she going psychotic?

Disturbed, as well as furious with herself for indulging in such a fantasy, she struggled to find her voice. "Who invited you?"

"You did." Valentin Kadar glared at her with those strange golden eyes, turned his back and took off.

What had happened? Angry, dazed, feeling as if she'd been seduced against her will, then thrown aside—and all without him so much as making a move toward her—she watched him disappear into the deep shadows of the buildings.

Then her pride took over and she turned to walk toward home. She told herself she'd felt desire, a craving more fiery and fierce than she'd ever experienced in her life, but she could have resisted Val if she'd wanted to.

Would she ever see him again? She wished she didn't care. He was mysterious, strange, sexy, arrogant... and definitely more dangerous than any man she'd ever met in her life.

Financially comfortable, if only for a few days, Eddie took the time to have a full meal at a diner before he made his way toward one of the few single-room occupancy hotels left along North LaSalle Street. He couldn't wait to crash, to clean himself up with a shower. Then he'd sleep all day.

The sky was growing gray in the east as he trudged down the sidewalk, his hand curled around the hundred-dollar bill in his pocket. Intent on his goal, he didn't hear footsteps until the man was upon him. Eddie eyed him warily.

"Tired, eh?" The question was tinged with a slight accent. "I expect you cannot wait to go to sleep."

"That's my plan."

"Mine, too... I want to see you resting long and peacefully."

Something about those words disturbed Eddie, though he didn't have time to so much as cry out before the man grabbed him and, with incredible strength, shoved him into a dark alley.

Pinned by the throat against a brick wall, Eddie still managed to croak, "Please!" His hands flashed out, one holding the precious money.

His attacker shook him. "Time is short and I have no mercy for useless peasants like you."

As the grip around Eddie's neck tightened, the hundred-dollar bill floated to the pavement....

CHAPTER TWO

The sun had set before Adriana awakened, her disoriented mind still tangled with memories of Valentin Kadar, her chest heavy with some unnamed emotion. She thought she might have dreamed about him—the reason she'd slept so long?—but she didn't want to explore the possibility too closely. Her imagination had run wild enough at dawn....

"Mr-r-row!"

Cat whiskers tickled Adriana's face, and she realized the weight on her chest came from a tangible source. "Phantom, I love you." She gave the cat a squeeze. "But not on top of me."

With a grunt, she moved her beloved pet to the mattress next to her. On the way home from work one morning a few months before, she'd found the young black cat wandering the streets—another lost soul. Adriana hadn't been able to resist saving the animal, and the cat had repaid her with affectionate devotion. Smiling at the quizzical black face split with a lightning bolt of white, she kissed the cat's furry forehead.

Which reminded her of Val. Heat flushed her cheeks as she thought about the kiss that hadn't been. Never before had her fantasies taken such a flight. Something about Valentin Kadar got to her in a big way. Even now, she could almost feel his presence. She could see his exotically handsome face—the golden brown eyes, high cheekbones, the wide, sensual mouth....

Her flesh pebbling at the mere thought of that mouth on hers in reality made her squirm. Determined to put Val out of mind, Adriana jumped out of bed and threw on a robe. But when she started to leave the bedroom, Phantom twirled around her legs.

"Sorry, sweetie girl, but you know Jen's rules."

Jennifer had agreed to let Adriana keep Phantom as long as the cat was confined to Adriana's bedroom and office.

Stumbling into the hall, she made her entrance into the living room. There on the couch, her sister, Jennifer, sat snuggled against her fiancé, Todd Grant, sections of the Sunday newspaper scattered around their discarded running shoes.

With a flip of her straight-cut brown hair, Jennifer gave her the evil eye and announced, "Ah, the queen arises at last."

Fighting annoyance at the nickname she resented and felt she didn't deserve, Adriana flopped into the chair opposite them. "Sorry. I meant to be up for brunch like I promised, but I didn't fall asleep until after eight."

"No wonder you refused to get up at nine." Jennifer didn't bother to hide her disapproval. "I did about everything to waken you but scream in your ear."

A fact that Adriana vaguely remembered. "Sorry." She meant it sincerely, knowing her sister's feelings were hurt.

"If you went to bed when you came home," Todd said superciliously, punching at his glasses with a finger, "you would have gotten up when you were supposed to."

A continuing argument between Adriana and three-quarters of the world—people who thought she was lazy because she couldn't work all night and do things she was *supposed* to all day.

"I don't think you really wanted to keep our date," her sister went on, "or you would have come home straight from work."

"I didn't go out with Irina, Jen. I merely walked home, and it took a bit longer than I thought it would."

"Walked?" Her sister's voice rose a notch. "At that time of the morning? Alone?"

Not wanting to share any information about Valentin Kadar—Jennifer would no doubt have yet another reason to show her disapproval—Adriana said, "I was perfectly safe." She knew that was her sister's main concern. "Plenty of other people were walking the street on their way home."

"Yeah, including a murderer," Todd informed her.

"Someone was murdered in *this* neighborhood?"

"God, I can't believe it!" Jennifer reached over to dig through the scattered newspapers. "Right on your route home from the club." She snatched up a section of the *Chicago Tribune* and waved it in Adriana's face. "Here it is. The guy was found in some alley only a few blocks west of Water Tower Place! His body was drained of blood."

One look and Adriana's throat constricted. Staring out from the front page of the newspaper was a sad face she knew well.

Eddie Szewicki.

Flipping on the safelight in his darkroom, Valentin Kadar stared at the photo in the rinse. The street musician's expression was riveting—despair combined with deep-seated fear—a perfect addition to his collection.

About to hang the print to dry, he noticed he had a visitor. A small gray bat hung upside down on the line.

"You again?"

In answer, the bat blinked and fluttered its wings.

Shaking his head, Val stepped over to the darkened window and raised the sash. He made a sharp sound through his teeth and pointed to the opening. With a squeak of protest, the bat roused itself, flew out of the darkroom and fluttered up toward the cupola where its family and friends gathered, gaining entrance through a broken window.

Though he was, indeed, lonely, Val knew he could have plenty of company if he wanted—the bats and owls and stray cats he felt compelled to feed.

Unwelcome night creatures such as himself.

But the only company he really desired was that of Adriana Thorn. No, he amended, the one he so desperately longed for was the *Daughter of the Night*. He preferred to think of Adriana as being one with her stage persona.

She'd definitely shaken his cynical expectations, although she'd been every bit as beautiful as he'd imagined. More important, she'd been even more lovely on the inside. A genuine person who seemed to want good things for others, he thought, remembering not only her monetary charity for the man she'd called Eddie, but her concern.

How unusual. Jaded, having lived in darker circles for far too long, he wasn't used to people being sincerely generous. Although he knew he should leave one such as her be, Val also knew he wouldn't. Inexplicably, she crowded his thoughts as no woman had done in years.

Hers was a siren call he could not refuse.

He pinned the wet print of the musician to the line, wondering exactly how friendly Adriana had gotten with the man in the past. They'd called each other by their first names. He'd recognized a real familiarity—perhaps a long-standing affection—in their manner.

Not that he would brood about the insignificant musician for one moment longer.

He had plenty to worry about, starting with the whereabouts of his family's enemy. He'd been tracking the bastard for years, and he was growing weary of this game. Undoubtedly thinking to fool him, his nemesis had left the old world for the new. But Val had followed. New York. Washington, D.C. Philadelphia. Now Chicago.

Each time he'd gotten too close, his foe had sniffed out his presence and had flown. And Val had had to start all over again. But no more. Chicago would be Armageddon.

Val was determined that here his adversary's flight would end forever.

"I can't believe Eddie came to such a horrible end," Irina lamented after hearing the bad news.

Adriana had introduced Irina to Eddie one morning when they'd gone out for something to eat after work, and they'd run into him several times. So she'd called her friend with the hope that talking to Irina would make her feel better.

"Irina, there's more..." She was gripping the receiver so hard that her knuckles hurt. "I was one of the last people on earth to see Eddie Szewicki alive."

Something she hadn't been able to tell her own sister. Then Jennifer would have freaked. Neither Jennifer nor Todd had any inkling that she'd actually been acquainted with the victim.

"You mean you saw him this morning?" Irina questioned her.

"On the way home from work."

"Omigod! How horrible. Thank goodness you're all right. The killer could have gotten *you.*"

Knowing that was only too true, Adriana assured her friend, "I wasn't alone."

"You weren't with anyone when you left the club."

"Not right away. Remember my telling you about this guy I met last night? He followed me and—"

"Followed you!" Irina interrupted. "How spooky."

"Yeah, I thought so at first..."

And maybe she should still think so, Adriana told herself. Where Valentin Kadar was concerned, she was a mass of confusion. As she was about Eddie for different reasons.

"I should have done more to help Eddie."

"You did what he would let you do," Irina said.

But Adriana was having a difficult time accepting that as an excuse. A person had a responsibility to her fellow human beings, especially the ones she knew and cared about. When she'd realized Eddie was so down and depressed, she should have gotten him the help he needed...she should have found a way to get him off the street.

But she hadn't.

"And now it's too late for me to do anything more for him," she mourned, her voice breaking. "Unless..."

"Uh-oh, unless what?"

"Eddie didn't have anyone, really." Realizing the bedroom had been thrown into deep shadow, only her small nightstand light on, Adriana glanced at the window. It was already after dark. She had always found something soothing about the night. She took a big breath, tried to calm herself. "I thought maybe I should go over to the SRO where he used to crash sometimes."

Adriana referred to the LaSalle, one of Chicago's remaining single-room occupancy hotels where some working poor lived on a week-to-week basis. Or, like Eddie, rented one of the furnished rooms for the night when he had the bucks.

"What will going there prove?" Irina asked.

"Maybe someone there knows of some distant relatives or friends to contact or something."

Eddie had always been far kinder to others than himself. Nonjudgmental, he'd listened to Adriana's problems a time or two when she'd been younger and feeling pretty mixed up herself. He'd told her to accept herself, insisted it was all right to be a little different. He'd assured her someday she'd be a success.

While he'd ended up sabotaging his own career and plunging to the bottom.

"Adriana, you're not thinking about going to that place by yourself at night," Irina was saying.

"I sure can't tell Jennifer."

Irina sighed. "Okay, that's why I'm volunteering."

Which relieved Adriana greatly. Irina really was a friend. Making plans to meet in an hour or so at Irina's place, which was on the way to the LaSalle Street hotel, Adriana felt a bit better. She rang off and headed for the shower.

Fifteen minutes later, refreshed and feeling a bit better, she was sitting at her vanity, blow-drying her long, thick hair, filled with a new sense of purpose...and the sudden sensation that she was being watched.

Jennifer?

Eyes to the door, thinking she hadn't heard it open because of the noisy blow-dryer, Adriana noticed the wooden panel was shut tight. Not her sister, after all.

Phantom?

Searching the shadowy room, she noted the cat was balanced awkwardly on a chair near the open window, intent on her own personal hygiene.

Knowing that no one could be spying on her from the outside—being that the apartment was on the sixth floor—Adriana tried to shake off the uneasy feeling and went back to her hair.

But the weird sensation wouldn't go away.

By the time her hair was dry, she was well and truly spooked.

And why shouldn't she be?

Eddie had been murdered just that morning, and she'd been one of the last people to see him alive.

She... and Val.

A shiver shot up her spine. She stared at herself in the mirror as if she were inspecting a stranger. *Val.* When Eddie had volunteered to see her home, Val had ordered him away and Eddie had complied.

A small voice of guilt told her that if she had insisted Eddie accompany her, he might still be alive.

Suddenly a movement pinned her gaze. She blinked, releasing the tears, and focused on the scene in the mirror. Behind her, Phantom stood near the open window. The cat was staring out into the dark, her fur fluffed up as if she saw something that frightened her.

But nothing frightening was reflected in the mirror.

Adriana whipped around to take a gander behind her even as Phantom yowled and made for the space under the bed. She blinked again as she thought she saw something pale flutter. She rose from her seat at the mirror and crossed to the window.

Standing there, staring out into the spring night, she had the oddest feeling that she wasn't alone. The hair along the back of her neck prickled. If she had fur, it might stand up along her spine, too. But try as she might, she saw nothing untoward.

Out on the lake, a tourist boat made its way north.

Below, hundreds of cars buzzed the drive.

Nothing unusual at all.

She convinced herself that her imagination was once again playing tricks on her. Then the cat must have picked up on her emotions and had been reacting to them. Even so, she grabbed a pair of trousers and an oversize sweater and headed for the windowless bathroom to dress.

And when she reentered the bedroom a few minutes later, she was apprehensive. No need. Phantom was once more ensconced in the middle of the bed, comfortably snoozing.

Adriana let go a sigh of relief and ruffled the cat's fur. "Silly puss!"

Then, swiping on some lip gloss, she grabbed her shoulder bag and left her room.

"Going somewhere *now?*" Jennifer asked incredulously.

Her sister was alone, dressed in a nightgown and sipping at some herbal tea. The newest pop-lit novel lay open in her lap.

Still a bit defensive from their earlier go-round, Adriana reminded her, "It's barely eight. You don't have to worry. I'm meeting Irina—"

"Take a taxi." Jennifer's tone was worried. "Please."

"Sure." Knowing her sister cared despite their time-clock and other differences, Adriana gave her a hug. "A taxi, it is." Then she left, double-locking the door behind her. If Jennifer had any clue as to what she and Irina were up to...

She took the elevator down and waved to Henry, the security guard, on her way out. Once on the street, she paused to catch her breath.

The winds whistled eerily like high-pitched voices around the century-old building, and a fog fingered its way up from the foot of the lake. Kind of spooky. Added to that, it was a dark night—the moon hiding behind a bank of clouds. An odd night fraught with tension. Reminded of Phantom's unusual actions earlier, Adriana swallowed hard, then told herself not to start imagining things again.

She started looking for that promised taxi. She was so preoccupied with that task, she didn't realize someone had come up behind her. Not until a linen handkerchief was presented to her with a flourish.

Heart thumping, she whipped around and came face-to-face with Valentin Kadar. The long scarf around his neck fluttered. It was white or cream colored, probably silk.

"You!" she said accusingly, her pulse racing at the very sight of him.

His sudden appearance was as odd as the night.

Staring into her eyes, he demanded, "Tell me what is wrong, Adriana. You are so sad." His own features were drawn into an expression of concern.

Still, his very presence put her on alert. "What in the heck are you doing here?"

"Looking for you."

The way he uttered those simple words shot a thrill through her. His light accent was as sexy as all get-out. As was the rest of him. Since she was wearing flat-heeled ankle boots rather than heels tonight, he seemed even taller than she remembered. More imposing. Almost... regal. He took her breath away. She swayed toward him.

Then suddenly snapped out of it. "I have to leave now." Before she forgot her purpose.

"Where do you go?" he asked, moving even closer so that she had to raise her face to look him in the eye. "What has upset you so?"

Val was still holding on to his handkerchief. He used it to dry the trace of a tear from her cheek. Feeling his touch through the crisp linen, Adriana was mesmerized. She couldn't move. A very physical longing filled her, reminding her of the imagined kiss....

Which forced her to renewed action. She swatted away the consoling hand and backed up a bit. Wildly, she looked around for a taxi, her effort in vain.

"I've got to meet someone."

"Another man?" he asked, his tone sounding too disinterested.

"No." Not that it was any of his business. "Someone I knew was killed this morning." When he didn't react, merely went on gazing steadily at her, she added, "You met him."

"The street musician."

Wishing he sounded at least a bit upset or surprised or something rather than so matter-of-fact, Adriana stated, "His name was Eddie Szewicki."

Though perhaps Val already knew that from reading the newspaper article. Could that be why he'd shown up unannounced, to console her? But how could that be, when he hadn't seemed to know why she was upset?

"A friend and I are going to talk to some people about what happened to him."

"You mean the authorities?"

She shook her head and eyed the empty, fog-limned street in frustration. Where was a damned taxi when a person needed one? While part of her longed to stay with Val, to allow him to comfort her with his mere physical presence, another part knew that she had to get away from him if she wanted to think straight. She *needed* to be able to think straight.

"You are not investigating this death yourself?" Val questioned her.

"Investigating?" she echoed. "I hadn't exactly thought of it that way."

What was she trying to prove? Adriana wasn't certain. She only knew she wanted to act. At a deep level, because he was another night person, someone who swam against the tide of daytime reality, she identified with Eddie. She didn't want him going to his grave unmourned . . . unknown, lost.

"Either you are investigating, or you are not," Val probed.

"I'm just going to see what I can learn about other people he knew with my friend Irina's help," Adriana said stubbornly.

"Your actions are foolish."

She bristled at his tone. He couldn't tell her what to do. "I wanted to do something for Eddie long ago. This is my last chance."

Frowning, he said, "But surely the authorities will alert the appropriate people."

"For a homeless person? You've got to be kidding." Then she weighed the fact that Eddie's death had been front-page news. "Though maybe, considering the circumstances..."

"What circumstances?"

"The way his body was found. Someone mutilated him, did something terrible to him."

Expression immediately closed, Val merely remarked, "Mutilated? This situation is definitely better left alone."

Left alone? Eddie shouldn't be alone in death. Not to mention that, underlying all, there was something more...

She focused on Val's scarf, fluttering once again in the breeze, and thought about the peculiar feeling she'd had in her room. She couldn't help imagining Val outside her window, while at the same time she knew such a circumstance was ridiculous. The sixth-floor window had no access.

Such a weird vision had to be spurred by something else, and she realized it was Val's coolness. She thought about the unfriendly way he'd handled Eddie last night, wondered if Val could have wandered back toward the park after he'd left her.

But surely paranoia was taking over. Val had nothing to do with the murder. She didn't want to think that she could be attracted to a man *that* dangerous.

Still, she fought a thrill of fear. "I want to ask some questions," she said, keeping her voice steady, watching his expression. "I figure maybe someone will know something about a bizarro who likes to kill people and mess up bodies."

His frown merely deepened. "Then I shall accompany you and your friend in your quest. This is no task for ladies."

She felt a bit relieved. If Val had done something wrong, he surely wouldn't want to be snooping around about it afterward. "Your company isn't necessary."

"I'm afraid it is."

The intensity she recognized in such insistence bothered her anew. The warning signals that had been set off at first sight of him tonight grew louder. Perhaps the very idea of talking about strange murders excited him.

"Forget it," she said, first backing away from Val, then rushing off as fast as she could go without actually running. "But thanks for the offer."

Adriana quickly found she couldn't shake off the man that easily. To her frustration, his easy, silent stride caught him up to her in seconds.

"I don't need your help," she protested, forcing herself to go faster.

He didn't reply, merely kept up with her as effortlessly as if he were flying.

She puffed, "Okay, so I don't *want* your help."

But he didn't respond to that, either.

She suddenly stopped short, as did he.

Catching her breath, she faced him directly and asked, "Do you ever pay attention to what people tell you?"

"If they agree with me . . . of course."

Adriana might have been tempted to dress the man down, but the streetlight above illuminated his sardonic smile. She suspected that, in his own odd way, he was teasing her. A real sicko surely wouldn't have a sense of humor.

"I am concerned for you, Adriana," he said, sobering. "I do not wish to see you put yourself in danger. And if you believe your actions tonight will honor your friend, then I shall respect that. Let me accompany you. I will honor him, too."

He spoke so sincerely, appeared so genuine.

How could she refuse? Tension drained from her limbs, and she had a hard time remembering why she'd been so determined to leave him behind in the first place. Besides, his manner was so charming, his accent so entrancing, his words melted her knees.

She sighed. "All right. Come with me, then." And added, "Just don't get bossy."

"Bossy?"

Thinking he might not understand the slang, she explained. "Pushy. Overbearing." Choosing to make herself perfectly clear, she added, "In other words—don't be telling me what to do." Jennifer and Todd already did enough lecturing. "I'm going to follow my conscience wherever it leads." As well as her gut-level feelings.

Which she hoped would eventually tell her what to do about Val. As they set off again, this time at a reasonable pace, she couldn't help being totally aware of him.

She felt guilty at the inappropriateness of balancing romantic attraction with grief for her friend's death, but she had to admit Valentin Kadar had gotten under her skin.

CHAPTER THREE

The LaSalle Hotel dominated several century-old graystone two- and three-flats to the north and was dwarfed by a modern steel-and-glass high-rise apartment building to the south. The four-story red brick structure was badly in need of tuck-pointing, and the window trim could use a good scraping and a fresh paint job. Hanging above the rickety door, a neon sign glowed a brilliant pink but for the final two letters.

"LaSalle Hot. Sounds like an adult video title," Irina joked, though her sarcasm had a real edge.

Adriana was aware that her friend was giving Val another sidelong once-over. Rather than being charmed by the Hungarian as Adriana had expected her to be, the usually irrepressible Irina had acted cool toward Val from the moment they'd met. Val had merely given her studied Gypsy look a scornful glance in return and had ignored her since.

"Let's go inside," Adriana said.

Val opened the door and held it for the two women. Irina slipped past him quickly, while Adriana lingered for a second, her gaze connecting with his, heat shooting through her from head to toes, before she entered. Even a sober occasion such as a friend's murder didn't shut off the appeal the man held for her.

The lobby was even shabbier than the exterior. Linoleum so worn you couldn't tell the original color covered the floors. Paint peeled from the walls. Dust motes visibly swirled through the air, challenging anyone with or without an allergy.

"This sure isn't the Ritz," Irina whispered.

An elderly man sat in a rickety lobby chair, head tilted back, mouth gaping open in a loud snore. Behind the scarred front desk, a bone-thin clerk sucked on a cigarette while he watched a wrestling match on an old TV with a bent antenna.

"Yeah, kill him, Thunderbuns!" he shouted.

Adriana shuddered that anyone should have to live in such depressing surroundings. Behind her, Val touched her arm lightly, as if he knew she needed encouragement. His very presence gave her more confidence.

So when the man behind the desk didn't so much as look their way, she cleared her throat loudly. "Excuse me."

The clerk kept his eyes on the tube. "Yeah?"

"Did you know Eddie Szewicki?"

That got his attention. He turned slitted eyes and a beard-stubbled face to her. "What's it to you?" He inhaled long and hard. "You a cop?" A cloud of smoke poured from his mouth and haloed his head. "I already gave a statement."

"No, I am . . . was . . . a friend of Eddie's."

"Hah!" the clerk barked, his gaze raking her expensive clothing in disdain. "Not a very good one or Eddie wouldn't'a been hanging around this dump."

"Speak to the lady with respect." Val moved closer.

The clerk started and frowned, acting as if he'd just noticed the other man's presence. "Yeah, yeah, sure, buddy," he agreed quickly, seemingly caught by Val's gaze. He blinked several times in trying to focus on her. "So what can I do for you, doll?"

Adriana sucked in her breath. Once again, Val's influence had worked its instant magic on demand. How did he do that? She gave him a quick glance, almost expecting to see him breathing fire or something, but his features were quietly unexpressive but for his intense gaze. In turn, Irina stared hard at the Hungarian, her mouth a straight line.

Shrugging, Adriana turned back to the clerk. "Do you know if Eddie had any relatives at all? Or other friends?"

"Sorry, I don't get intimate with the clientele. I check them in, take their money, hold their mail—"

"Did Eddie get mail from anyone?"

The clerk pulled a face. "Not so I remember."

"That pretty well eliminates relatives," Irina remarked. "At least, any we can find fast."

Adriana feared she was right. "What about friends?"

The clerk stuck the cigarette in the corner of his mouth when he said, "He knew people here."

"Anyone special?"

"Kid named Louis Brock—another *musician.*" Disdain colored the title.

"We should find this Louis, then," Val said.

Adriana nodded. "But first, do you know where they took Eddie?"

"Ever hear of the morgue?" Eyeing Val speculatively, the clerk quickly added, "Over on West Harrison."

"Choice neighborhood," Irina muttered.

Though she figured she would hit a dead end here, Adriana asked, "Did the police give you any details that weren't in the newspaper report?"

"Yeah, me and the cops are best friends.... Uh, meaning no disrespect to you, miss," he quickly added when Val took a step closer.

"Then you don't know anything about how or why he was killed?"

The clerk barked another laugh. "No more than that the murderer musta been some loony-tune who escaped the nut factory. Thought he was a vampire and sunk his teeth into old Eddie's neck."

Adriana felt Val tense next to her, and noticed Irina's eyes widen. "A vampire?"

Ash from the clerk's cigarette wafted down to the counter. "Nothin' but a dried-up husk...that's what one of the cops said. And fang marks stabbing into the throat."

With that, the guy turned back to the wrestling match, while Adriana and Irina exchanged spooked glances. At the same time, the sound of feet came clunking down the hotel stairway and a young man in his late teens or early twenties appeared. He had curly blond hair and was carrying a beat-up guitar case.

The clerk tore himself away from the television long enough to inform Adriana, "You hit the jackpot, doll—there's Louis Brock now."

Giving the man a thank-you he paid no attention to, Adriana moved toward the musician. Val shadowed her so close she could feel his breath feather her hair. Her pulse raced like a locomotive. What was it about him that got her all stirred up?

She tried to put her attraction out of mind as she concentrated on the young man, who looked vaguely familiar. Undoubtedly, she'd seen him play somewhere. She introduced herself and her companions and told Louis they'd come about Eddie. He suggested they sit a minute. The old guy who was snoring woke up, gave the small group descending on him one look through bleary eyes and stumbled toward the stairs.

Adriana and Irina sat across from the musician. Though Val remained standing behind them in the shadows, she was fully aware of his presence.

"We were as good friends as could be, considering the circumstances," Louis was saying. "What happened to Eddie... God, no one should die like that."

Adriana agreed. "Then you'd be willing to go to some kind of service for him?" An idea that had occurred to her.

"You bet. You just tell me where and when and I'll show."

"What about other people? Do you know of any out-of-town relatives? Other friends? We kind of lost touch lately."

"I think he had people in Ohio somewhere. I could find a coupla musicians who'd want to pay their last respects."

"Great." Adriana was feeling a little better. Her quest hadn't been in vain.

"I was always telling him to be more careful of who he trusted," Louis was going on mournfully, his brown eyes sad. "He shoulda listened better."

"Do you refer to someone in particular?" Val asked.

The young musician gave a start. He obviously hadn't noticed Val. "I don't know if it means anything, but I saw this guy give him money a coupla times in the past week or so. He slinked around. Know what I mean? Kinda weird?"

"What did this man look like?"

Louis shrugged. "Hard to tell. He always wore a big brimmed hat and a dark trench coat with a cape thing attached."

"Have you told this to the police?" Val asked.

"Sure. The detective in charge scribbled something in his little notebook, but I doubt he'll sic the force on this guy."

"Why not?"

"Where you been, man?" Louis gave Val an amazed once-over. "We got a disposable society, you know? If a human being don't make some big contribution, where all kindsa people get stirred up over his death, his case gets a once-over—just so the cops can say they did something—then pushed into a file drawer. One of those unsolved mysteries, like on television."

Louis Brock was too young to be so cynical, and yet Adriana feared he spoke nothing but the truth. Hadn't she told Val as much herself? Still, she reminded herself, finding a bloodless body wasn't an everyday occurrence and so it had to get some attention.

"Listen, when we set up some kind of service, how can I let you know?" Adriana asked.

"Call here. I'll get the message...if I'm still around. Me and my friends are real uptight about this situation."

Adriana said, "You should keep to populated areas, shouldn't travel around alone at night." Thanking him, she led the way out of the hotel.

"Well, now we can go home," Irina said, sounding relieved.

Adriana shook her head. "Not yet. First we have to go see Eddie."

"You want to go to the morgue at this time of night?" The redhead sounded incredulous.

"I want to make sure they don't...dispose of him...before we can set something up. If you want to go home, though, I understand."

"And let you go alone? No way!"

"She will not be alone," Val reminded Irina, moving in on Adriana purposefully. Her breath caught in her throat as his long fingers closed about her wrist.

"Uh-huh." Giving the Hungarian another narrow-eyed look, Irina came up on Adriana's other side. "Let's get going."

Fog slithered along the south branch of the Chicago River, helping to camouflage the boat that was illegally docked outside a deserted warehouse. All was quiet, for it was barely 10:00 p.m. By midnight, the place would be teeming with life.

Low life, Miklos Rakosi thought, chuckling to himself as he watched his men getting ready to set up.

For it was from the dregs of humanity that he earned his lucrative living. The numbers runners, the drug dealers, the pimps—they all came to him. Not that he interfered with their businesses. He had no need to tangle with organized crime. Nor to incur the wrath of the gangs that ran Chicago's inner-city neighborhoods. He merely provided a service. Entertainment. A floating craps game.

By dawn, he'd be a little richer. And he'd be gone from this place like a wisp of the fog that was crawling up the sides of the *Buckthorn.* He never held a game on consecutive days, nor in the same place twice in a row. His days of the week varied as did his locations. Sometimes he even went as far south as Indiana. That way, he didn't have to worry about any vice squads getting a secure bead on him.

He had enough to worry about with Valentin Kadar hot on his trail once more.

He thought of the medallion he always wore, the reason Kadar was after him. The metal and stone that gave him certain abilities...and that would keep him safe from evil that walked the dark centuries. Kadar would never get the medallion... not as long as he was alive.

"Hey, boss, anything I can do?" asked Zeke, his personal bodyguard, as the burly man returned to the deck from the head.

"Yes, something important." Miklos took a slip of paper from his breast pocket. "Find a phone and make a call for me."

"Sure. So who do I talk to?"

"The authorities."

Incredulous, Zeke asked, "You want me to call the cops?"

Knowing it went against the grain for a man who'd spent his entire adult life evading contact with the police, Miklos ran his thick fingers lovingly over the missive before he handed it over. "You will make an *anonymous* tip about a vicious crime, and you will read what I've written here."

Circling his massive hand around the medallion, the reminder of who he was, Miklos Rakosi renewed his determination to do whatever was necessary to stop Valentin Kadar from endlessly pursuing him, once and for all.

Waiting to identify the body, Adriana, Irina and Val stood in a small, sterile room with a big window and no furniture.

"This place gives me the creeps." Irina glanced at Val furtively, no doubt including him in the statement.

Adriana was a little more than curious as to her friend's reaction to Val and couldn't wait to get the redhead alone to question her. Normally a person who gave strangers the benefit of the doubt, Irina was going against type where Val was concerned. Though Adriana did remember Irina getting irrational about a waiter at the club one time, claiming he had "bad vibes." She'd even insisted Frank fire the guy.

"We won't be here long," Adriana said. Her head was a bit light and she was having a little difficulty breathing.

"At least we don't have to go into one of those rooms with the bodies stuffed in drawers like they show in movies."

No, the closest they would get to Eddie would be the glass window, thank goodness.

Irina gestured. "There he comes."

The attendant who was working with them wheeled a stainless-steel cart carrying a wrapped burden before the window. Adriana closed her eyes as she realized Eddie lay in a body bag. The attendant unzipped the material. Adriana nearly choked. One look at the caricature of the gentle face now puckered and shrunken without blood was enough. She focused on a spot on the floor, aware of Irina's quick intake of breath.

"I didn't know how difficult it was going to be."

"Wherever Eddie is, he appreciates your caring," Irina said. Then she stiffened. "Hey, how did *he* get in there?"

Adriana looked up, shocked when she saw Val on the other side of the window, standing mere inches from the body. She hadn't even realized he'd disappeared from the viewing room. And how had he gotten where he didn't belong? The attendant named Wendell had been specific about that being impossible.

At the moment, he was turned away from Val, clipboard in hand. He checked his watch and made an entry on a form.

"What's Kadar doing?" Irina asked, voice trembling as Val bent over the corpse.

"I don't know." A bit in shock, she stared at Val. He was removing the sunglasses he'd worn since arriving at the brightly lit morgue. His face glowed pale under the fluorescents. "Getting a closer look at the marks on Eddie's neck, I think."

And as the attendant set down the clipboard, Val slipped the dark glasses back on and melted away, unnoticed. Wendell zipped up the bag and rolled the cart back out of sight.

"So where did Mr. Creepy disappear to?" Irina asked.

"He's not creepy," Adriana protested, even while silently admitting that Val had inspired the same reaction in her a couple of times. "He's just different. European."

"He's more than that, Adriana."

"Right, he's Hungarian."

"Still more. I have this strong feeling . . ."

"Feelings can be wrong." Adriana didn't want to hear any psychic predictions, especially negative ones about a man who attracted her so. She had enough doubts of her own to fight. "This is such a horrible, eerie situation, it's easy to feel creepy about anyone."

But Irina hardly seemed to be listening. "Kadar. I know I've heard that name somewhere—"

The redhead's statement was cut off by the door opening behind them. Both women turned as Val reentered the room. Again, Irina stiffened. In contrast, as so often happened when she was near him, Adriana seemed to melt a little, felt the blood pulse through her veins, making her want to draw closer. A bit breathless, she was about to ask Val about his illicit actions, when the attendant poked his head inside, as well.

"You can come with me now."

A few minutes later they were seated around the morgue employee's desk, Adriana between her two companions.

"So you want to make arrangements to dispose of the remains?" Wendell asked. "The coroner already did an autopsy."

"I'd like to plan some kind of service, certainly. Where will Eddie be buried?"

"Potter's field. Unless you actually want to claim him and bury him elsewhere," Wendell said. "But I'll warn you that's gonna cost you a pretty penny. We're talking thousands here."

"I don't have that kind of money."

Not after Stone had skipped out on her, damn him, taking everything of value, including her cash-station card. He'd emptied her savings, and it had taken her the several months since to make enough money to replace her basic CDs and stereo equipment. She was only now starting to replenish her resources. Not wanting to see Eddie buried in potter's field, though, she was actually thinking about scaring up the credit to give him a proper burial elsewhere.

Before she could say so, Val told Wendell, "Money will not be an object."

Realizing that he was offering to pay, Adriana was a little shocked. "You didn't even know him."

"But I know you." He removed the sunglasses again, and his golden gaze drove into her. *I know you.* "This would make you happy?"

Caught, she again went breathless. "Yes, but—"

"Then it is done." Taking out a pen, he scribbled his name and address on a piece of paper—he lived in Uptown, a mid-north neighborhood that was crawling out of its decades-long collapse, she noticed—and handed the information to the attendant. "When he can be released, you will find me here."

Wendell looked over the information. "No phone number?"

"I have no phone."

The attendant frowned. "Hey, we don't do door-to-door."

Val caught his gaze and held it. "You *will* find me," he stated, his voice convincing. "I will make the trouble worth your while."

And when Wendell responded, "Worth my while," as though hypnotized, Irina grabbed Adriana's arm, her long nails biting into her flesh through the sweater.

Freeing herself, Adriana made a face at her friend. Irina was wearing an I-told-you-so expression. One Adriana chose to ignore. Val's generosity for a stranger got to her. What was left of her former doubts retreated completely, taking a back seat to deep gratitude.

The interview over, they all rose. Irina headed straight for the door. Feeling light-headed, Adriana swayed. Val steadied her, his hand on her arm making her knees weaken further.

"You are all right?"

"Fine," she promised. "I just can't remember the last time I had a meal." After hearing the news about Eddie upon awakening, she hadn't even thought about food.

"Then you must eat. I shall see to it personally."

A thrill shot through her at his tone. "Great. I know lots of late-night places," Adriana said as they joined Irina, who seemed edgy, restless.

"I hope the taxi's still waiting," the redhead said, then glowered at Val. "Although *you* could probably conjure one if you gazed out into the night hard enough."

"You speak to me?" Val asked, his voice cool.

Irina drew herself up to her full petite height. "I'm the seventh daughter of a seventh daughter. I know certain *things.*" And she added, "You have no power over me."

At that, Val laughed. "I shall keep that in mind, little Gypsy."

At least he wasn't taking Irina seriously. Having thought about inviting her friend to eat with them, Adriana thought again. Irina and Val were like water and oil—they just didn't mix. And she didn't need any more of her friend's strange, vague warnings while she was with the man. Irina didn't usually mix fortune-telling with day-to-day life. She would have to talk to the other woman when they were alone, find out why she was so freaked.

But for now, she could only think about one thing—being alone with Val.

Maybe the man did have special powers....

Adriana Thorn was a special woman, one Val knew he should stay away from. Still, a few minutes after letting her annoying friend off at her apartment house, he found himself seated across from Adriana in a late-night place a few blocks from her home, a fancy Gold Coast version of a steak-and-egger. They were tucked into a shadowy corner in the back of the room.

"I'm sorry about Irina," Adriana said. "You probably think she's rude."

He appreciated such sensitivity, rarely encountering people who worried about his thoughts and feelings. "It was a painful evening for both of you."

"Well, I'm glad you understand. She's not usually like that."

Val removed his sunglasses to gaze freely at the woman who fascinated him. She was not wearing her work disguise tonight. Her face was clean of makeup, the well-scrubbed look giving her a touch of innocence he hadn't expected. Her clothing was simple, the deep red sweater revealing one enticing shoulder. Her skin was flawless, he noted, his gaze tracing a very slow, very erotic line to her sensual mouth, hesitating when it reached her lovely neck....

Then their waitress arrived, cutting off his view as she poured two cups of coffee. She set down the insulated pot and pulled her pad and pen from her apron.

She asked Adriana, "What'll you have?"

"Scrambled eggs and hash browns with pancakes."

"Bacon or sausage?"

"No, thanks. I don't eat meat."

"How about you, honey?" the waitress asked Val, who was slightly amused by the endearment.

"Steak and eggs—the eggs sunny-side up—"

"And the steak?"

"I prefer very rare. Ask the chef to merely touch each side to the grill."

Unable to hide a grimace, the waitress made a note on her pad, muttering, "Steak, still walking."

She hurried away and Val concentrated on Adriana. "You are a vegetarian?"

"Since I was a kid. I eat dairy products and fish, but I never developed a taste for blood." She sighed. "Which reminds me of Eddie. What an awful death. Killed by some maniac who thinks he's a vampire."

"Eddie wasn't killed by a vampire." Noting her startled look, he went on, "I examined his throat. The marks were not from teeth or fangs."

"How did you get into that room, anyway?"

He was thankful she hadn't questioned him further about his knowledge of murder and pathology. "I opened the door. The attendant didn't notice."

"You can really sneak around if you want to."

"I am light on my feet," he agreed, watching her pour cream into her coffee, sip at it, make a face and reach for the sugar.

"I didn't mean for you to pay for Eddie's funeral, you know."

"It's nothing."

She stirred the sugar into the coffee. "Yes, it is." Her large gray eyes told him how much she thought of the gesture. "It's very kind. And I wouldn't have let you take the responsibility if I had the money in the bank. If you give me a little time, I can pay you back."

"That will not be necessary, I assure you." The money was nothing compared to the anticipation of seeing her a little happier than she was now.

"I actually had the money until a few months ago. Until that creep Stone ripped me off."

Unsure of her meaning, he repeated, "Ripped you off?"

"Stole my cash-station card and withdrew all my savings." She took a sip of coffee and added, "Not to mention that he also took my CDs and stereo equipment. And most importantly, the special mixes I had produced for my work."

"And you know the man who did this?"

"Stone Drake. He and I were . . . close."

"The man you loved," Val guessed, his mood darkening at her sad expression.

"Thought I loved," she corrected. "He was a performance artist and a great actor. He fooled me good, I'm ashamed to admit. Here I thought I was a pretty good judge of character. I wouldn't have given the real man the time of day."

"Perhaps you are too trusting." Another indication of her innocence of the real world, at odds with the sophisticated facade she presented. Sensing her pain, Val said, "Someone should find this Stone and give him what he deserves." He would like to see all the unhappiness in her life erased.

"What a creep. I can't stand someone pretending to be what they're not."

Something he recognized as discomfort registered. Afraid that Adriana would somehow see through him if they kept on in this vein, Val was relieved when the waitress interrupted with their food. She set his plate before him. The steak was swimming in its own red juices, the very sight fueling his suppressed appetite.

"Whoa, that's rare, all right," Adriana noted, looking away from his plate to her own pancakes and eggs.

Val took a pouch from his pocket. Opening the mouth, he gathered some of the dried ingredients between forefinger and thumb and sprinkled them over the steak.

Adriana glanced up. "What in the world? You carry your own seasoning?"

"Paprika—I am Hungarian, you know. And there are herbs mixed in that aid in digestion."

"A stomach problem, huh?" She appeared sympathetic. "You have a lot of stresses on you?"

"More than I would like," he said truthfully.

"You need to do something about simplifying your life before you get an ulcer."

Though he knew that the solution wasn't so simple, Val definitely agreed he needed to take action, to make certain he found Miklos Rakosi as soon as possible. Not that success would change what he was. He took a big, satisfying cut of the rare meat, sopped up the juices, then savored the taste.

"I'd have thought getting involved with photography would help your stress level," Adriana was saying between bites of her eggs and potatoes. "Is that your business or hobby?"

"I have no need to work for money," Val admitted. "But when a man has too much time on his hands, he can go a little crazy. Years ago, I used to paint, but I find photography much more fascinating. Photographs reveal so much." Sometimes he thought of his shots as crystallized reality.

"They reveal things about people?"

"About all night creatures, including people. Perhaps one day you will allow me to shoot you."

Her sensuous lips curved into a smile, made his excitement level rise. Her effect on him was instant and urgent. He tried to calm himself with another bite of the steak.

"I'll make you a deal," she offered. "I'll let you...if you let me come along on a shoot."

He swallowed. "This is possible."

"Great." The smile broadened. "So what are you going to do with all these photographs you've been taking?"

He heard a low throbbing, a steady beat...her pulse? His own? And he warned himself to take care. He wanted what he couldn't have. What he couldn't allow himself.

"I'm preparing for a show that opens next weekend at Night Gallery."

"I know that place real well. It's connected to the Full Moon Café. I go there sometimes, to the poetry slams. To listen to the readings, that is."

To Val, a believer in destiny, it seemed that they'd been fated to meet one way or the other. But why? To torture him? Being around Adriana Thorn would be exquisite torture, he had to admit, but that made it no less painful.

He couldn't allow his desire for her to take him from his chosen path.

He couldn't slip back into his old ways.

The thought that he might be tempted beyond endurance worried him as they finished their meals, ate at him as he walked her home. He couldn't allow his true nature to take over, not with her.

As they neared the lake, he concentrated on the fog, the delicious wisps of translucency that writhed around their legs and slithered up their bodies. He envied the mist that tasted hers.

And as they paused in the shadow of the trees flanking her apartment house, when he could no longer clearly read the innocence of her well-scrubbed face, he weakened. She was no longer Adriana Thorn, the woman of compassion and generosity, but the Daughter of the Night, an exotic, shadowy creature who flirted with the same darkness he knew so well.

"When I'm near you, I can feel the pulse of the universe," he said, turning her toward him.

"Poetry, again. You're something else, Val Kadar." She sighed, an inviting whisper on the night. "No man has ever made me feel this way before... so reckless."

Her warmth under his hands invited *him* to recklessness. He sensed the blood rushing through her, faster and faster. Compelling. Dizzying. The thunder of her heart called to his own. Teasing. Tempting.

He wanted her. To taste her. To drink in her very essence and make it part of him.

"Valentin," she murmured, swaying toward him, slipping her hands up his chest to touch his neck.

The temptation was too great. Constant. Irresistible. Even for a man with an iron will such as his own, the conclusion was inevitable.

He lowered his head, his mouth first searching out that lovely, graceful throat. She arched her neck, easing his foray. He laved her skin, sucked at the tangy hint of salt. Breathed deeply of her scent, perfumed with female musk.

His blood rushed faster. He wanted—no, needed—more.

But something inside still forbade it.

His conscience? Did he really have one after all these years?

He forced his head higher, to where her sensuous mouth awaited. Parted. Moist. Seductive. The might of his passion was too great. He paused. Took a deep breath. Visualized what could happen if he let go, which he didn't want to happen. Fever tempered, he took her only when he knew he could control the driven part of himself.

Even so, the moment their lips met, he was in ecstacy. As he tested her mouth, his imagination ran rampant, so that he had to curb himself from exploring too far.

She murmured against his mouth—faint, inviting sounds. He reeled with wanting her. Contented himself with the texture of her lips. Lush like ripe fruit, ready for the plucking.

Suddenly a salty taste in his own mouth made him stop. *Blood.* In his passion, he had accidently nipped her. With a growl that came from deep within, he set her from him. "Get inside before it's too late."

Her eyes were dreamy as she obeyed, starting to move away. Yet she found the strength to pause, to object, "I don't understand."

He caught her gaze. "Go inside," he said again, speaking more gently. "I've ruined too many other lives."

That awakened her more fully. She blinked rapidly, her feathery brows drawing together. "What are you talking about? Other women?"

If that would do. "Yes. I am not good for you."

And then he turned and walked away.

They'd both escaped this time....

CHAPTER FOUR

Even awake, Adriana almost felt as if she were dreaming, Valentin Kadar playing the central figure in her romantic fantasies.

The following afternoon, running some errands at Water Tower Place, the several-story indoor shopping mall on Michigan Avenue, Val was constantly at the back of her mind. She couldn't help recounting the time she'd spent with him, especially the kiss they'd shared. She was certain this one had been for real, and it had been better than anything her imagination could produce. Even recounting the embrace made her pulse throb.

And her lip.

She ran her tongue over the slight nick and imagined she could still taste Val.

She couldn't wait to see him again.

A small part of her wondered how she could be so focused on a man she'd only met two days before, while another part found her bond to him to be the most natural thing in the world. Val had said he knew her. Now she felt as if she knew him, too, in some deep, inexplicable way...as if their very souls had touched. Undoubtedly his willingness to put himself out for a man he hadn't even known had affected her more deeply than she might have imagined.

Wondering if he'd heard from the authorities about Eddie, wanting to make some plans for the burial service, she was frustrated that she couldn't call Val. In this day and age, she couldn't figure out how anyone could get along even for a few days without a telephone. But perhaps he'd gone somewhere else to call her. Too restless to wait the ten minutes it took to walk home, she found a pay phone and called her answering machine to pick up any messages.

The one she got was a bitter surprise.

"Hi ya, lover. It's me."

Adriana froze. She'd recognize that voice anywhere—Stone Drake.

"It's been a long time," Stone said, his voice deep and scratchy—undoubtedly practiced. "Too long. Maybe we can get together...and discuss how badly you want your mixes back." He laughed softly. "I'll be in touch."

Furious, Adriana stood there, staring at the telephone, even after the answering machine cut her off. She'd thought she would never hear from Stone again, and now he called out of nowhere to make some kind of deal about the mixes he'd stolen from her.

How dare he!

"Excuse me, but if you're done with your call..." an elderly woman said.

Heat shot up into her face. "Yes, of course. It's all yours."

Upset enough to need someone to talk to, Adriana was frustrated that Irina was unavailable. Irina had called that morning to warn Adriana not to see Val again—and then she'd said she'd be visiting one of her aunts on the southwest side. And Adriana really didn't want to discuss the situation with her sister, who might be less than sympathetic.

Then it hit her. Val could be understanding. She needed to talk to him, anyway... about Eddie. And, deep down, she needed to see him, no matter that he issued warnings about ruining other women's lives. She would make sure that he didn't harm hers in the least. Besides, he was gracious and generous, sexy, yet polite and protective. Nothing like Stone.

Compulsion ruled. Remembering the address he'd written down for the morgue attendant, she left Water Tower Place and headed for the nearby subway stop. The sun was just setting, its last golden rays apparent on the horizon. That she could be talking to Val within a half hour lightened her mood. Only when she entered the rapid transit station did she realize she'd been a bit too quick on the draw. Rush hour was over and the hordes of daily commuters were long gone. Perhaps she should have taken a bus. The station was nearly deserted but for a few unsavory characters.

A couple of teenagers wearing gang colors eyed her from the other end of the platform. And nearby, a man woke from his drunken stupor, fixing his bleary gaze on her.

"Got a quarter, honey?" he slurred before slumping over once more.

A city person through and through, refusing to let circumstances stop her from doing what she wanted, Adriana was nevertheless careful as always. She wore the strap of her shoulder bag crossed over her chest and resisted appearing intimidated, knowing that looking like a target could very well make her one.

Still, she was relieved when the train thundered down the tunnel to stop before her. The doors whooshed open. And her stress lessened slightly as she entered her car. Within minutes, the train hurtled out of the underground tunnel and up onto the elevated tracks. Adriana stared out the windows. A gray pallor had already settled over the city that was metamorphosing at the end of another day.

But rather than anticipating the approaching night, Adriana fought renewed tension when she left the train at the Lawrence Avenue stop and headed west on foot. The unfamiliar neighborhood—one that had a long way to go before regaining its polish of decades before—put her on guard.

Unused to the uncomfortable feeling, Adriana rushed along, one hand hanging on to her bag, the other to her skirt, which fluttered under the onslaught of a gusting wind.

She ignored wolf whistles coming from a low rider. Turned onto Broadway, passing a hooker hanging around the curb, her wares on display in a miniskirt, thigh-high boots and a leather jacket.

A couple of doorways later, she dodged a man who popped out, calling after her, "Hey, sugar, I can sell you something to put a smile on that pretty face."

She raced across Broadway and onto a side street where, block after block, signs of gentrification were intermixed with evidence of neglect. Having assumed Val was living in one of the rehabbed buildings, she was shocked when she came to what she remembered as his address.

Staring at the towered Victorian building dominating the dark gray sky, she couldn't imagine the impeccable and moneyed Valentin Kadar living in a place even more derelict than the SRO. The gray-stone facade was crumbling. The paint trim was cracked and peeling.

Several windows were boarded up. And the surrounding double lot was littered with papers and plastic that played tag with the errant breeze.

The house honestly looked as if it hadn't been occupied in years.

Adriana thought back to the morgue and concentrated. She could almost see the piece of paper with the address in Val's hand. Yep, this was the place, all right.

Reluctantly, she advanced on the house. The wooden steps groaned under her weight, and an eerie wind whistled around the pillars of the rotting porch. A chill shot down her back, and she wrapped her jacket closer around her. Being that it was nearly dark, she expected to see some welcoming light from within. But the latticed windows that weren't boarded up showed no signs of life.

So why did she feel as if she were being watched?

Adriana glanced around behind her. The street was quiet, deserted but for the parked cars. Still, the weird feeling wouldn't go away. Imagining she caught a movement from one of the vehicles, she stared harder.

Nothing.

Nerves buzzing, Adriana turned her attention back to the house and approached the entrance, but she could find neither a nameplate on the mail slot nor a bell. And before she could knock, another gust of wind swept over her...and creaked the door open, making her start.

When her pulse steadied, she peered into the shadowy interior. "Hello? Valentin?" She waited for a moment and stepped inside the hall entryway, noting the neglected inlaid wood flooring underfoot. "Hello? Is anyone here?"

Curiosity drew her into the large, nearly empty room to the left. Eyes adjusting to the gray gloom, she checked out the decor—an antique couch and upholstered chair edging a worn oriental area rug, and a spindle-legged end table supporting a glass-and-brass lamp with a fringed cloth shade. An old-fashioned radio graced the elaborate carved wood and ceramic-tiled fireplace that smelled of recently burned logs. Flanking the radio were half-melted candles. More candle holders embellished the various nooks and crannies familiar to old Victorian homes, while overhead, a bulbless crystal chandelier collected dust.

From somewhere nearby, she heard a scrape....

"Valentin?" she called softly, her heartbeat accelerating at the thought of seeing him.

Still no answer.

Either she'd imagined the noise...or the wind had caused the old wood to creak. Val probably wasn't even here.

Feeling a bit odd about roaming around someone's home without his knowledge, she nevertheless couldn't bring herself to leave just yet. Instinct drove her to learn more about Valentin Kadar. She passed the broad staircase that led to the upper floors and checked out the formal dining room. The last of dusk's gray light shimmered through latticed windows, several of which were cracked.

The room was empty but for a stack of unpacked boxes.

How curious. She couldn't imagine a man like Val would be content to live in such disarray. Of course she could hardly believe he lived in this house—or this neighborhood—to begin with.

A clattering behind the stacked boxes made her pulse jump. A second later, out popped a raggedy gray cat that, taking one look at her, ran for the nearest doorway, one she assumed led to the kitchen.

"Oh, kitty, don't be scared," she called, thinking to go after it. But undoubtedly any pursuit would panic the poor animal, so she stopped herself.

That Val had a cat pleased her inordinately. Wondering where he'd gotten himself off to, about to retrace her steps to the hallway and leave, she noticed a half-open door on the other side of the staircase. Somehow, she'd managed to miss this entrance to another room. Sensing that questioning eyes followed her—the cat, no doubt—she approached the opening. She was standing before it, torn between exploring further and leaving, when another creak too loud to be made by a small animal came from directly behind her.

Before she could so much as look over her shoulder, a hand grabbed hold of her arm and spun her around. Her pulse jumped, yet she expected to see Val rather than coming face-to-face with a total stranger.

"Who the hell are you?" she demanded, her heart pounding against her ribs. Tearing her arm free, she backed away from the hard-looking man, who was wearing a mean expression. "And what are you doing in here?"

"I could ask the same of you." He reached inside his cheap suit jacket, making Adriana fear a gun. But all he brought out was a leather case. He flipped it open, displaying a badge. "Detective Carmine Panchella—Chicago Police Department. And you are?"

Relieved that she hadn't interrupted a thief or worse at work, she sagged. "Adriana Thorn. And you nearly scared the stuffing out of me."

"I was looking for the owner of this shack. A Mr. Valentin Kadar."

"You have found him" came a familiar voice from above.

Startled, for she hadn't heard his approach, Adriana turned away from the detective to see Val watching her from the middle of the staircase. He was wearing what could pass for an old-fashioned smoking jacket—quilted black velvet trimmed with a deep red—and his hair was mussed as if he'd just awakened. Thinking about Val stretched out in a bed, Adriana experienced an intense longing that she didn't want to examine too closely. She was hard-pressed to shake the feeling off.

"There you are," she said, a bit breathless. "I thought I came all the way out here to find you and then you weren't even home. Though I did think it was odd that you left your door open. You should be more careful. Hungary may be safe, but Chicago isn't." Fearing her nerves were making her prattle, she fell silent.

"Adriana, welcome to my home." Staring into her eyes, Val descended the remaining steps and joined her. He found her hand, raised it and sensually touched her flesh with his lips. Only then did he turn his gaze to the stranger. "Detective, what can I do for you?"

A grimace that passed for a smile briefly crossed Detective Carmine Panchella's hard features. "I came to ask you a coupla questions about Eddie Szewicki."

"Perhaps we should sit."

Val led the way through the deepening gloom into the living room. He took the lone upholstered chair and Adriana sat on the end of the couch closest to him, while the detective took the other end. Unbuttoning her jacket, she slipped it off but let the garment encircle her shoulders since the house was chilly and didn't seem to be heated.

"Now what is it you want to ask me?"

"Uh, it's kinda dark in here," Panchella complained as he whipped a pad and pen from his jacket pocket. "Think you can scramble up some light?"

"Certainly."

Val reached out and switched on the lamp, which pooled the sitting area with a glow so soft that Adriana guessed it to be less than forty watts. Either Val liked living with sparse furnishings in the near dark, or he'd been too busy with his photography and the family matter he'd mentioned to take care of his own comfort. Not that he appeared to be having any trouble seeing. His gaze roamed purposely across her dark green pleated blouse. In response, her breasts tightened beneath the thin material.

Oblivious to the tension building between her and Val, Panchella asked, "That's it?"

Without taking his eyes off her, Val softly replied, "I can light candles."

"Big help. Never mind. I'll try the braille method here." The policeman flipped open his notebook. "We got kind of a curious call down at the station late last night." He paused a second before casually saying, "Someone suggested we talk to you about Eddie Szewicki's death."

Attention on the policeman, Val crossed his legs and relaxed against the back of the chair. "Someone?"

"An anonymous tip. So why would anyone want to give us your name?"

Adriana watched the detective doodling on his pad of paper, as if he were pretending to be taking notes. Coming to Val's defense, she told Panchella, "Probably because we were asking around about Eddie last night." Surely the police didn't suspect him because of a crank call. "First at the SRO where Eddie bunked some nights, then at the morgue. Didn't this anonymous caller mention me?"

"Nope—though I am aware of your activities, Miss Thorn. The two of you and the Murphy woman. Me and the morgue attendant Wendell compared notes before I came to see you. That's how I got this address."

"Your point, Detective," Val said, his tone growing impatient.

And Adriana could swear Panchella was squirming in his seat.

"I'm gettin' to the point." He took a big breath first. "Okay—so this nut case said something wild about a vampire being on the loose and that we should talk to Valentin Kadar 'cause he would know about it."

Mouth open, Adriana could barely contain her anger. What was it with this vampire business? Did everyone think Eddie's death was some kind of joke?

"A vampire?" To her relief, Val presented the detective with a completely straight face when he said, "Surely a rational man as yourself doesn't believe in such an untenable explanation for the poor man's death."

"Me? Nah. Of course not."

"The marks on Eddie's neck were not made by teeth or fangs of any kind," Val went on. "The holes were precise...smooth...as if made by a metal or perhaps a plastic instrument. An unusual weapon to be sure."

"So the medical examiner told me." Panchella slitted his eyes at Val when he asked, "But how did you know all that, Mr. Kadar?"

Wondering if Val might not get himself in trouble by admitting he'd checked out the body personally, even though he wasn't supposed to have gotten near it, Adriana was relieved when he said, "To think otherwise would mean that *I* believed in vampires."

Both men smiled, their expressions that of two resourceful opponents.

Then the detective sobered.

And Adriana tensed when Panchella said, "On the other hand, Mr. Kadar, you'd also know about the wound site if you were the killer."

"If I *were* the killer, Detective, wouldn't I be a bit foolish to claim the body?"

Panchella thought a moment. "Okay, makes sense," he conceded, barely pausing before pouncing once more. "So why did you claim the body? You and Eddie good friends?"

"I'd barely met the man."

Noticing the gray cat was lurking in the shadows, its complete attention on Val, Adriana said, "He did it as a favor to me, Detective. I knew Eddie for some years, and his death was so upsetting—"

"Ah, so *you* knew him."

And Adriana found herself in the unenviable position of having the detective's full attention trained on her. She shrank back into the corner of the couch. "He was the roommate of a former friend."

"And you saw him last . . . when?" He'd stopped his doodling and was now taking notes for real.

Adriana swallowed. "The morning he died. Eddie was in the park by the Water Tower, playing his violin for contributions." Which sounded much more dignified than panhandling.

"You were alone?"

"We were together." Val now sounded as if he were coming to *her* defense. "I walked Adriana to her home."

Adriana's realization that he'd conveniently skipped the part about having followed her and catching up to her when she'd been talking to Eddie made her a little uneasy. A movement from the shadows distracted her train of thought, however. The cat slid along the chair, and as if recognizing its silent presence through some sixth sense, Val dropped his hand and stroked the animal.

And, despite the serious situation, Adriana wished he were stroking her.

"So you were both in the vicinity," Panchella was saying. "How long before he died?"

Val's sardonic smile slid into place. "I could only know that if I killed him, Detective."

"Good answer."

Picking up the cat, Val uncrossed his legs and stood. "Will that be all?" His body language clearly stated that, as far as he was concerned, this interview was over.

"For now." Detective Panchella took his time getting himself together and to the door. "But let me give you two some friendly advice."

"And what would that be?" Adriana found herself asking in a none-too-friendly way.

"Neither of you think about leaving town soon."

"We have to bury Eddie first," she said coolly, standing next to Val and absently fingering one of the cat's silky ears. She almost felt as if she were touching *him*. "Can you tell me when that might be?"

"I'll give the medical examiner's office the high sign." He opened the door to the night—it was already after dark. "You can claim your friend's remains first thing in the morning."

"Thank you."

Adriana broke the tenuous connection with Val, moved to the door and watched the detective rush down the stairs and to his car. Then she realized Val was watching her. Warmth spread along her limbs and through her center. She didn't turn away. She wanted Val's golden gaze on her. Wanted something far, far more tangible from him...and an elusive something that she suspected might be unattainable.

Shaking away the renewed longing she'd experienced all morning, she chose to satisfy her curiosity about the latest development in Eddie's murder. "Can you believe someone made a crank call to implicate you?"

"People often do strange things."

He said it so calmly. She was surprised that he didn't seem to share her sense of righteous indignation. "But who?"

Val was stroking the cat, the sensuous action threatening to mesmerize her.

"It could be anyone," he said. "Someone I offended...even the killer himself."

She tore her gaze away from Val's hand and the animal who was purring loud enough to be heard. "That would mean you know the killer."

He shrugged. "Or that he knows me. Or perhaps he merely obtained my name from the morgue attendant in hopes that he could throw off the authorities."

Thinking about being implicated in a murder, Adriana rubbed the sudden gooseflesh from her arms and realized she'd left her jacket on the couch. "It's a bit chilly in here."

"Is it? Cold doesn't bother me. Perhaps I should turn on the heat."

"That's all right," she said, making for the couch. "By the time the radiators get hot, I'll probably be gone."

"Pity." He sounded both disappointed and resigned. "But then I have some things I must take care of myself tonight."

Biting back disappointment—part of her had wanted Val to insist she stay—Adriana slipped the jacket over her shoulders.

The cat meowed and Val said, "I think this fellow needs some food. If you'll excuse me a moment..."

"I'll come with you. I love cats and have one of my own. What's his name?"

Val led the way through the dining room. "He has not told me."

"Excuse me?"

The sardonic smile touched Val's lips. "I meant that I do not know his name."

"You mean you didn't give him one?"

"He doesn't belong to me." Still holding the cat, Val kept going, right through the dining room into the dimly lit kitchen whose appliances seemed nearly old-fashioned enough to be original to the house. "I merely feed him along with several of his companions."

"But you let him inside."

"He let himself inside, probably through a basement window. Not that I mind."

Noticing the cat had placed his front paws on Val's shoulder, and that he was pushing his head at Val's face, Adriana smiled. "I'd say he thinks he belongs to you."

"We have an understanding."

He set the cat down, opened the back door and grabbed a bag of dry cat food from its resting place on a windowsill. Adriana followed him onto the rear porch where a tabby waited in the shadows. No bulb in the porch light, but one could see well enough under the yellow glow provided by the huge lights in the alley. The moment cat crunchies hit one of the several bowls laid out along the building, the striped cat darted forward, competing with the gray.

"There's enough for everyone to feed," Val scolded the hungry animal softly. He filled a second bowl, then another.

Adriana heard a plop and turned to see a filthy red-and-white cat vault the rickety railing. A calico came running from the opposite direction. By the time the half-dozen bowls were filled, they were all occupied.

Warmth threaded through her. She pictured Phantom when she'd found her pet, could remember clearly how emaciated the poor kitty had been. A couple of the alley cats were nearly as thin, but it was obvious they wouldn't be for long under Val's generous care. The strays were properly appreciative, a few even looking for affection along with the food. At her very vocal demand, Val ran his hand up the calico's spine and tail, the cat arching and giving him a look that could only be described as adoring.

Adriana was experiencing a bit of adoration herself at the moment . . . as well as amusement. If Val thought these cats didn't belong to him, he had another think coming.

He replaced the bag of cat food on the inner windowsill, and she helped get fresh water for the animals. A new arrival—a young black cat, maybe half-grown—wound itself around Val's ankles. He fluffed its fur and gave it a pat in the direction of the food bowls before heading back inside.

He closed but didn't bother to lock the back door. Adriana thought about suggesting he do so. Somehow, she suspected he might laugh at her cautionary advice.

Instead, she said, "It's kind of you to care for all those strays."

He shrugged off the flattery and stepped close enough so that she could feel his breath on her face. "I have an affinity for lost creatures of the night."

Adriana thought he might be even more of a night person than she. "You identify with them?" she asked, unable to tear her gaze from his.

"At times . . . yes. And taking care of any living creature helps me a little, helps makes up for—"

He didn't finish the statement and he sounded so sad, almost miserable.

"Makes up for what?"

A lonely existence? Adriana was tempted to place her arms around him and tell him he didn't have to feel lost and alone anymore. Somehow, looking into his lean, chiseled face, she didn't think he would be wholly appreciative of her sympathy. Everyone had his pride, and she suspected Valentin Kadar had more than most.

"You seem so very sure of yourself," she said instead, keeping her tone lighter than the wellspring of emotions flooding her. "Too sure to feel lost, certainly."

"There are many ways of losing one's self. Some less pleasant than others."

She had no idea of what he was talking about and wasn't certain she wanted him to explain. His gaze dropped to her mouth. He raised his hand. Ran a thumb over the lower lip that was still slightly swollen from his too-intense kiss of the night before.

Her pulse quickened. She felt as if she'd been stung. Not that he hurt her. More like made a connection. Electricity. No, darker. Something even more elemental and human. A stirring from the depths of her soul.

CHAPTER FIVE

"Forgive me," Val whispered, his expression serious.

"For what?"

"This."

The pad of his thumb lightly traced the nick on her lip. She felt it again, stronger this time. A primal heartbeat. Her lashes fluttered and the room seemed to shift slightly. Her head grew light as if she'd had a bit too much wine, and she hadn't even been drinking.

She swayed toward him, and for a moment thought Val might take her in his arms and reacquaint her with his embrace. Her body quickened. Her breasts tightened. And a flush crept through her.

He moved his hand slowly, surely, tracing the line of her jaw, the length of her throat, the curve of her shoulder. Her breath grew shallow. Trembly. He didn't stop until he'd pushed her jacket aside and found her heartbeat through the thin material of her blouse and the aching flesh of her left breast.

"We're beating as one," he murmured, his face pale and serious.

"What do you think that means?" Mesmerized, she wondered if she should fight the feeling that enveloped her thoughts.

He didn't answer. Merely gazed at her with a look so intense her pulse rushed in response. She was awash with heat. Damp. Her knees began to melt.

And then Val very deliberately broke the connection. Removing his hand. Turning away from her. Leading the way back through the house.

Suddenly feeling foolish at her overblown reaction to him, Adriana backed off mentally.

Val stopped at the staircase, opened a door that hid a closet beneath the steps and traded the quilted jacket for a designer model, the kind she was used to seeing him in. He ran a comb through his hair, slicking it back, then found his sunglasses and slipped them into a breast pocket.

"I'd better get going," she said.

"You have a vehicle?"

"No. I took public transportation."

"But you will take a taxi home." He opened the door for her in true gentlemanly fashion. "I shall see to it."

She exited the spooky old house, biting back the caustic reply about being able to take care of herself that hovered around her lips. In truth, she wasn't so certain she *could* always take care of herself—at least, not where he was concerned. She'd never met a more compelling, more mesmerizing man. Certainly not one who got to her so deep so fast.

Compared to Valentin Kadar, Stone Drake was amateur-hour stuff.

Stone.

Remembering that the message her former boyfriend had left on her answering machine had been her initial impetus for seeking out Val, Adriana realized she wouldn't be talking to him about Stone. At least, not now.

And somehow, with Val's hand on her arm, guiding her down the rickety front steps, Stone's double-dealing seemed less important than it once had.

Night cloaked the city streets, camouflaging many of their faults. The neighborhood felt more inviting. Even Val's home appeared less decayed than it had in the daylight. Maybe she felt more at ease because she was so comfortable with the dark, in some ways truly the Daughter of the Night.

Only one discordant note bothered her. Again the feeling of being watched. A glance over her shoulder assured her no one was on the street. Shrugging off her uneasiness—something Val obviously didn't share—she headed east.

"I thought we should figure out what to do about Eddie's burial," she said. And still wondered about his willingness to pay the expenses.

"I have contacted a funeral director who agreed to prepare him for burial immediately." Val asked, "Eddie was Catholic, was he not?"

"Yes. How did you know?"

"His last name. Good, then. I have made the correct arrangements—a plot at Saint Boniface Cemetery, a few blocks from here." He pointed straight north.

Adriana was happily surprised. "Have you contacted a priest, too?"

Even under the streetlights, she could see the shadow cross Val's features. "I leave that and the other specifics up to you."

That was more than fair and something she really wanted to do for Eddie. "I don't know what church he went to, but I'll find a priest from somewhere. Since we don't even know if anyone will be there but you, me, Irina and Louis, I thought we should keep things simple—maybe have a grave-site service."

"I shall do my best to be there for you."

Adriana's mouth fell open. She hadn't considered his not being there. Then again, he hadn't known Eddie. "I understand."

"No, you do not, but that is expected."

Perhaps she didn't. Adriana mulled over this news. For some reason, she hadn't considered Val's not being present at the service. She was oddly disappointed. But why should she be? Val had gone further out of his way for a stranger than she'd have expected of anyone.

He'd even gone to the morgue with her....

"The marks on Eddie's neck," she said, remembering his conversation with Panchella. "How did you know they weren't made by some kind of an animal?"

"The holes were too perfect," Val answered, his tone indicating his displeasure at her bringing up the subject. "Teeth would leave a jagged wound."

The very idea leaving Adriana feeling queasy. "Whoever killed Eddie must be really warped. I mean, draining a person's blood isn't a normal criminal activity. Who would do an awful thing like that?"

Her gaze met Val's, but she was not comforted by the experience. He seemed ... cold, withdrawn to the point of remoteness.

"Various cultures throughout the ages believed in blood sacrifice," he said. "They thought to mimic nature herself, where there are predators and prey. Something must die so that something else may live."

Adriana's stomach turned even though she was quite familiar with the facts of nature and knew something about history. "I don't care what people did in the past—we're not living in the Dark Ages here. And we're not beasts. Anyone who would suck all the life's blood out of another human being, even using a modern instrument of some kind—no matter the reason—is just plain sick!''

If she expected him to argue with her, he didn't. Instead, he stated, ''Indeed, there are terrible diseases, Adriana. Some that affect the soul, as well as the body.''

''What are you talking about? Mental illness?''

But he made no reply as he slipped on his sunglasses, holding himself rigidly and definitely apart from her—as if he chose to ignore her existence.

What in the world had happened? Certain Val felt the same disgust at the way Eddie had died that she did, Adriana couldn't understand how an invisible wedge had suddenly been shoved between them.

She didn't have long to think about the situation, however, for they'd reached Broadway, and Val stepped into the street to hail a taxi for her. The driver pulled over to the curb with a screech of brakes.

''Your vehicle,'' Val stated without emotion.

She tried staring into the eyes that had held her prisoner less than an hour ago. She imagined that, behind the dark glasses, they appeared cold. Dead. He'd closed himself off from her. An unacceptable situation.

''Val, what's wrong?''

''It is late. You must be going.''

He was using that voice on her, the annoying one that got other people to do his bidding. A flash of frustration kept her from being equally inveigled. She ignored the taxi.

''Not until you tell me what's going on here.''

''I have business to take care of—as I told you before.''

''I don't mean that, and you know it,'' she argued, noting a hip-looking young man dressed in black leather jogging down the street straight for them. ''What happened here? You're acting as if we'd just met or something. No, not even that! You came on to me when we met."

Val's lips were set in a straight line, and his jaw was clenched tight. The garish streetlights accentuated his pallor. His expression and stance made him appear tough and mean, totally unlike the man she was getting to know. Before she could wring an explanation from him, the guy in the leather duds sped by them and stopped before the taxi.

Panting, he threw open the rear passenger door. "I need to get to—"

Quick as lightning, Val shot out a hand and stopped him from completing his sentence. Fingers of steel latched on to the stranger's arm and spun him away from the vehicle. The taxi driver hiked around to see what was going on.

"Hey, do I got a fare or not? Somebody make up your mind or I'm getting outta here and finding a paying customer!"

"This is the lady's taxi," Val told him coldly. "You will wait for her." Then he turned to his quarry. "You get your own."

"And you get stuffed!" His features pulled into a nasty expression, the young man slashed Val's hand away. "The lady wasn't going nowhere that I could see. And I'm late for an important appointment. She can take the next taxi that comes along!"

The guy tried approaching the cab once more, but, face a fierce mask of anger, Val acted even more quickly than before. This time, his hand connected with the stranger's throat, stopping him cold.

"Val!" Adriana said anxiously.

But Val ignored her. "I said this is the lady's taxi." He was practically lifting the man off the ground by his neck. "You can get the next one."

What in the world was wrong with him? First he'd withdrawn coldly from her, then become furious with a stranger. He'd always seemed to get what he wanted with his softly spoken commands. She'd never experienced his temper before. And while he'd gotten her guard up a few times, she'd never sensed this capacity for violence.

A frisson of fear crawled up her spine.

Toes of his boots doing a strange tap dance on the pavement, the stranger was making gagging sounds and prying at Val's fingers and wrist to no effect.

Worried that he would actually hurt the guy, Adriana begged, "Val, please, let him go."

She touched his arm, felt the muscle like steel ungiving beneath his suit jacket. This wasn't the Val who'd paid for a homeless musician's burial. He wasn't the man who fed and comforted stray cats. He wasn't anyone she knew. Or wanted to know for that matter.

Her voice trembled when she pleaded with him, "It's only a taxi, for heaven's sake."

Making a harsh, guttural sound that raised the hair on the back of her neck, Val lifted the leather-clad man and threw him as if he weighed nothing. Limbs flailing, the stranger shot back into the corner building, colliding into the brick wall with a thud.

Then, hands at his throat, he staggered off, croaking, "You're crazy, buddy!"

"Val, what's wrong with you?" Adriana demanded, even as he herded her into the back of the taxi.

"Take this lady home," Val said, handing the now nervous-looking driver money.

"Yeah, sure, pal, whatever you say."

But he didn't say anything more, merely closed the door and watched as the taxi shot off down Broadway. Confused, her heart sinking, Adriana turned around to find Val staring after her. The thrill of fear clashed with the memory of something equally potent. How could he have turned from her dream lover into her worst nightmare in the space of minutes?

Then traffic got in the way and Val simply disappeared into the night.

"I wish you wouldn't disappear like that," Jennifer complained the moment Adriana walked through the door. She was curled up in a chair, studying the day's stock report.

Having assumed her sister would be tucked into bed, Adriana realized her stressful evening hadn't ended yet. "Oh, God, dinner." Another planned shared meal missed. "I'm sorry." Doubly sorry because she hadn't eaten, the fact probably making her even more edgy.

"I don't care about dinner. I left some stir-fry and rice for you on the stove."

"You're a doll, Jens." With that, Adriana attempted her escape. "Thanks."

"Not so fast. Isn't there something you'd like to talk about?"

Adriana stopped in the kitchen doorway. Where to start? Her meeting Val? Eddie's death? Being looked upon with suspicion by the police? Learning a man who could mesmerize her one minute could make her shake in her shoes the next? But Jennifer couldn't possibly know about any of that.

"Like?" she asked, letting her sister take the lead.

"Stone Drake."

"You listened to my messages?"

Adriana had her own line installed when she'd moved in with her sister. Her phone and answering machine were in her bedroom and they had a strict policy about respecting each other's privacy.

"I couldn't exactly help it," Jennifer said defensively. "I was home and the cat was squalling, so I decided to see what was wrong with her. All Phantom wanted was some attention, so I gave her a few pats and let her have the freedom of the apartment for a while." She pulled a face. "Stone called while the door was open."

Expecting a lecture, Adriana braced herself. "Then you'll know I didn't ask him to."

Sighing, Jennifer rose from her chair and crossed to the kitchen doorway where Adriana still stood.

"I know Stone hurt you when he did his disappearing act, and now he's trying to hurt you again. You're my sister, Adriana, and you should be able to tell me what's going on with you, even if you think I won't like it. Please, don't hide things. Don't hide your feelings from me. So I don't always approve of you—I know you don't always approve of me."

"Jens—"

"C'mon, don't try to deny it. It's a fact. Our parents must have gotten one of us from space aliens or something. But just because we're different doesn't mean we can't be there for each other."

The backs of Adriana's eyes stung. She'd been feeling alone when she didn't have to. She put her arms around her sister, and Jennifer gave her a comforting squeeze. She should have known better. Despite her lectures about Stone, hadn't Jennifer been the one to insist Adriana move in with her so that she could feel safe again?

"So you want to talk about it?" Jennifer asked.

Adriana pulled back and searched her sister's face. "Not about Stone, no, but there's something else..."

"Let's get you something to eat first."

A few minutes later, sitting at the kitchen table, Adriana cautiously told Jennifer about Eddie, keeping the details to a minimum, fearing to push this newfound closeness. She skipped the trip to the SRO and morgue and merely said she was helping to make arrangements for Eddie's burial and service that would be held the next day, if possible.

"Why didn't you tell me you knew him when you saw the newspaper article?"

Swallowing a mouthful of vegetables and rice, Adriana made a face. "Guess."

"Well, I wouldn't have assumed you were personally involved with the guy's death."

"I wasn't, though I spoke to Eddie on my way home. Val and I were possibly the last people to see him alive." Adriana realized telling her sister was inevitable. "Don't be surprised if a Detective Carmine Panchella comes to call."

"Omigod!" For a moment, Jennifer looked horrified. Then her expression changed, and she said, "Val?"

"A man I met at the club."

"You're dating someone and you didn't tell me about that, either."

"We're not dating...exactly. I mean, we are attracted to each other," she said, wondering what Jennifer would think if she admitted that she was pretty much obsessed with a virtual stranger. "But with Eddie's death and all..."

"You haven't exactly had time to develop a relationship," Jennifer finished for her. "So tell me about this Val."

Uh-oh, now they were in dangerous territory. Adriana chewed on the last of her food. No way would she admit Val alternately spooked her and turned her on. No way would she tell Jennifer that he must have been following her home the night Eddie died. She would stick to the easy stuff.

She swallowed and said, "His name is Valentin Kadar, he's from Hungary, and he's a photographer."

"Newspaper or portrait?"

"Um, more like art," Adriana reluctantly admitted, knowing her sister hadn't been too fond of some of her artist friends in the past. "He's going to exhibit at a local gallery."

If Jennifer had any negative vibes, she hid them behind her cup of tea. "So he's good?"

"I don't know. I haven't seen his work yet." No photographs had been in evidence in Val's home. She hadn't realized that until this very moment. How odd. "I only met him a couple of days ago."

"So is he handsome?"

About that she could be totally honest. "Drop-dead gorgeous."

"And nice, I hope."

"He has his moments," Adriana said, the incident with the taxi suddenly foremost in her mind.

Not that she was about to mention Val's scary temper to Jennifer, either. She wasn't about to push this open-door policy between them.

"When am I going to meet him?"

"I couldn't say."

She couldn't even say if she would ever see him again. He obviously wasn't planning on coming to the service for Eddie, and after their strange interaction earlier, she wasn't certain he would seek her out again. The idea that he might be out of her life for good tore at her. His putting her on edge once in a while seemed a small price to pay to be near him. As for the hint of violence... now that she thought about it, she was probably blowing the incident out of proportion.

Either that or she was doing one hell of a job of rationalizing.

Jennifer yawned loudly. "Boy, I'm pooped."

"It's way past your bedtime."

"Mm." Rising, she said, "Will you do something for me? When you figure out what you're doing tomorrow—the service for your friend, or whatever—just leave me a message as to where you'll be so I don't worry."

"Sure."

"Good." Stifling another yawn, Jennifer kissed her cheek and left the room.

Adriana cleared the table, though she put off cleaning up the sink. It was getting late and she had several calls to make. She planned to contact Irina and Louis once she found an open-minded priest willing to officiate over the burial of a nonparishioner. Hoping that wouldn't be too tricky, she pulled out the telephone book from the hall closet and retreated into her bedroom.

Phantom was curled up in the middle of the bed, waiting for her. No sooner had Adriana closed the door behind her than the cat stretched and yawned aloud.

"So you escaped your prison for a while, did you?" She sat on the bed, stroked the animal's silky fur. "Making a convert of Jennifer?"

Phantom purred her response, reminding Adriana of the gray stray that had gotten into Val's house... reminding her of Val.

Closing her eyes for a moment, she imagined she was in his kitchen with him. She imagined he was about to kiss her. As had happened then, longing for him filled her. Even forcing herself to think about the way the evening ended so badly didn't lessen her craving to be near Val.

Had he put some sort of spell on her, or what?

"Phantom, what am I going to do about that man?" she murmured, staring into the cat's green eyes.

"I did what you wanted, boss," the narrow-faced snitch said when he showed up on the *Buckthorn* late that night. "I parked myself some ways down from Kadar's spook house just like you told me. He never knew no difference."

Leaning back in his leather upholstered chair, Miklos Rakosi fingered the medallion and stared at the man who hadn't earned the nickname Weasel for nothing. "Well done." The snitch would have a heart attack if he realized the full danger he'd been in. "And did Kadar have official visitors?"

"Besides the woman, a suit showed just like you said he would."

"What time was that?"

"Sunset."

Rakosi hid his disappointment. The call had been placed the night before. What had taken the police so long to get their act together? He'd fantasized about them breaking the door down and trying to drag Kadar out of bed. There would have been a terrific battle. More troops would have had to be called in. But, with luck, Kadar might have gone to jail first thing that morning. That would have stopped his adversary from coming after him—possibly for good.

"Did the detective take our friend in for questioning?" he asked, thinking Kadar might have tried to be agreeable.

"Nah, the suit left alone."

So the anonymous call hadn't been taken as seriously as he'd hoped . . . though the situation had been checked out. That was something, he supposed. Obviously, the authorities needed more incentive before they would take action.

"And then what happened?" Rakosi asked, wishing he could take some sort of action himself. But he valued his own skin too much to face his adversary alone.

"A while later, Kadar left with the woman."

The woman again. Who was she? "And you followed them?"

"From a distance. Kadar put her in a taxi after having a ruckus with some bozo. Strong bastard. Could never tell by looking at him, that's for sure." Weasel's narrow face pulled into a puzzled frown. "Then he kinda just disappeared on me."

No surprise there, Rakosi thought. Something made him demand, "His companion—describe her."

"Kinda exotic. Long purply red hair. A real looker."

"Kadar does like his women . . ." Rakosi thought hard, his memory suddenly producing an image. "I think I know who she is. I've seen him with her myself. Though I don't know her name." But he moved on to the more important action of the moment. "I want you to keep watching Kadar and his house. See what goes on there."

Weasel appeared wary. "Uh, you mean all night? Alone?"

So the man did sense his enemy's power. Rakosi went on, "The police may have the place under surveillance, as well. If so, you will need to be careful of them. But I want to know everything they do. Kadar himself will probably not return until dawn," Rakosi said reassuringly, knowing his enemy's modus operandi nearly as well as his own.

Then he waved the man off to do his bidding. The snitch slinked away like the weasel he was. And Rakosi settled down to consider his options. All of them.

Including figuring out a way to use the woman to his advantage.

CHAPTER SIX

Getting a late start and speeding toward Saint Boniface Cemetery in a taxi, Irina asked Adriana, "You didn't let Kadar, um, take advantage of you, did you?"

This after Adriana admitted she'd spent time with Val the night before. Staring out into the gray that followed sunset, she echoed, "Take advantage?" Merely talking about Val had started her fantasizing about being with him. Better than dwelling on their current purpose of burying Eddie.

"You know," Irina was saying tensely. "Did he do anything weird?"

Eyes widening at the implication, Adriana shook away her distraction and turned to her friend. "Since when did you become a prude?"

"I didn't mean that—well, yes, I guess I did. That and other, more dangerous things."

Part of Adriana only wished Val had taken advantage of her. "If I had gotten more deeply involved with Val, it would be my own business."

"Adriana, I'm serious."

Reminded of the potential for violence she'd recognized in the man, Adriana demanded, "And what *dangerous* things?" Surely Irina couldn't know anything about his temper—Adriana hadn't said a word about how the evening had ended. "What is your problem with Val, anyway?"

Irina made a squinchy face, then announced, "He doesn't have an aura."

"What?"

"An aura. Yours is usually warm. Red with tinges of gold. He doesn't have one... like he's doing something purposely to block my being able to see it."

Unable to take her friend too seriously—Adriana wasn't certain she believed in auras or any of the myriad other metaphysical subjects that interested Irina—she tried humoring her. "Maybe you didn't look hard enough."

"I'm the seventh daughter of a seventh daughter," Irina reminded her. "I would know whether or not Valentin Kadar has an aura. And believe me, he doesn't!"

"All right, calm down."

Glancing at the driver, who was from the Caribbean if his accent could be trusted, Adriana realized he was watching them through the rearview mirror. She was uncomfortable that a complete stranger seemed so interested in her personal business. She tried bringing an end to the disturbing discussion.

"So he doesn't. So he's different. I don't mind, okay? Now let's drop it."

But Irina was like a dog with a bone. "He's different all right. Adriana, I have this feeling about him. I think he may be into black magic."

Once more reflected in the mirror, the driver's eyes widened.

And Adriana was becoming exasperated. "Irina—"

"Hear me out, would you? I talked to my Aunt Ludmilla about him yesterday. The mere mention of the name Kadar was enough to alarm her."

"Why?"

"She was certain she'd heard it before in some negative context, though her memory isn't what it used to be."

"That's certainly startling enough information to condemn the man."

"Don't joke. She was very troubled. She said she'd talk to her Hungarian friend, Sofie, and get back to me."

"I don't understand why you're doing this," Adriana said as the taxi pulled into Saint Boniface.

"Because you're my friend and I care about you."

Adriana took a big breath. "Well, thank you for that."

The exasperation faded away and she was reminded of why she liked the redhead so much. In addition to being fun and charmingly peculiar at times, Irina was warm and caring, and Adriana had always been appreciative of the fact.

The taxi stopped near the rose-bedecked grave site where a handful of people, including Louis and the priest, already gathered around the raised coffin. Searching for some sign of Val, Adriana was highly disappointed.

"Omigod, look who's coming," Irina said, pointing to the driveway on the other side of the grave site.

Adriana wondered if she could be seeing things. Through the gray pallor of evening, she recognized her sister and Todd. "I don't believe it!"

"I thought they didn't know about Eddie."

"I decided to tell Jennifer last night."

When her sister had asked her to leave a message as to where she'd be, Adriana hadn't expected Jennifer meant to show her this sort of support. Her eyes stung with unshed tears, but she was uncertain if her sister's being there for her was responsible, or if her reaction to the reality of Eddie's death was finally catching up to her.

"Irina, you have to promise me something."

The redhead eyed her suspiciously. "What?"

"That you'll keep your thoughts about Val to yourself when you're around my sister and her fiancé."

"But—"

"Promise."

Looking decidedly unhappy, Irina said, "Oh, all right, I promise." She jerked open the door and left the taxi, adding, "But I'm not done with you!"

Heaving a sigh of relief, Adriana settled with the driver. "Here you go. Keep the change."

He took her money, saying, "You be listening to your friend, lady, if you know what be good for you." Concern was etched on his weathered features. "She has the *gift.*"

Startled by the unexpected advice, she said, "I'll keep that in mind," figuring that he'd brought his island superstitions with him and so had been inspired by Irina's commentary.

Even so, the advice followed her to the grave site, where she forced it aside to shake the hand of the priest who'd been liberal enough to officiate at the service, and to overlook some of the usual formalities of a Catholic burial. Louis quickly acquainted her with Eddie's musician friends, while Adriana introduced Jennifer and Todd.

"Thanks for coming," she told them all.

Jennifer gave her a sisterly hug, and for once Todd actually smiled at her.

"My friends and I thought maybe we could say a special last goodbye to Eddie," Louis said, indicating the musical instruments stacked behind them. "If you don't mind, after the padre here is finished, we could play something we think he'd like."

Tears gathered in Adriana's eyes. "That would be wonderful." Having gotten her wish, knowing Eddie would not be lowered into the earth unmourned, she gave the priest a watery smile. "I guess everyone who's coming is here." Though, obviously, not the man who'd paid for the burial. And darkness would soon settle over the graveyard. No use in waiting. "Father, would you please begin?"

"Certainly." He opened the leather-bound book in his hands. "Let us pray..."

Adriana concentrated on finding comfort in the priest's words. Within moments, however, she became distracted by the feeling of being watched. She took a quick look at the people around her—all focused on the priest.

But her neck hair was definitely prickling.

She searched the deepening gloom, eyes passing over the spread of elaborate headstones and winged monuments. Eventually, she glanced over her shoulder and across the road. Then she saw him—a darker silhouette against the murky gray of twilight.

Her pulse leapt with excitement.

Val had come, after all.

Irina's warning and the taxi driver's advice—both tried to intrude... both forgotten in an instant.

Filled with a joy she wouldn't have thought possible at so solemn an occasion, she turned back to the service and focused on the priest's words, content that neither Eddie nor she had been forsaken.

* * *

Val knew he could not forsake Adriana Thorn merely because her truth had come harsh upon his ears. He recognized qualities in her that he envied. Qualities that he vaguely remembered as having had himself once.

Honesty.

Loyalty.

True caring.

The priest finished with a blessing, and three men and a woman picked up their musical instruments. Studying the small group of mourners, listening to the heartfelt piece they played over the casket, Val almost envied the man inside.

Who would mourn him?

Not that his passing was a consideration. Certainly not anytime soon. Hopefully, not before he had the opportunity to make up for the dark deeds haunting him, perhaps thereby finding a way to save his very soul.

He stared at the striking woman, whose rich mahogany hair looked like blood pooled against the white of her jacket. A breeze swept through the old tombstones, ruffling Adriana's collar and teasing the hem of her ankle-length white skirt so that he got a glimpse of her well-turned calves. She was so hauntingly attractive that it was difficult for him to believe that she was equally kind and generous.

She is the one.

Something told him she could help him, this woman who called herself the Daughter of the Night. Even as he thought it, something that he'd believed was gone forever flickered in his cold breast. *Hope.* He couldn't change the past, but the future was a clean slate, and a future with Adriana Thorn in it was certainly more appealing than the bleak existence that had become his curse.

He was drawn to her, and like a moth to a flame, he chose to chance life.

"Eddie's life on earth might be over, but now he's with God," the priest said, squeezing Adriana's hands.

Eyes awash once more, she nodded. Plucking a single dark red rose from one of the baskets adorning the grave, she stroked the velvet petals as she strolled with him to the road. "Thank you for everything, Father."

Holding his leather-bound prayer book to his side, he moved off, following the path the other mourners had taken. Cemetery workers respectfully waited in the background to finish their job, while Jennifer, Todd and Irina stood in a small knot nearby.

Stepping forward, Jennifer hugged her again. "C'mon. We'll take you and Irina home."

Touched that her sister was trying to make things easy for her, Adriana was also aware that Val was waiting. "Um, I can't go just yet."

"You can't hang around here," Todd said, slinging an arm around her sister's shoulders. "It's almost dark."

"I won't be alone."

She glanced toward Val, who hadn't moved from where she'd first spotted him. He was so incredibly handsome and virile looking with the wind ruffling his dark hair and fluttering the lapels of his jacket. Their gazes connected, and a flush of anticipation dissipated some of her sadness.

"Is that the Hungarian?" Jennifer asked, raising a brow.

"That's him, all right," Irina offered, falling silent when Adriana glared at her.

"Maybe we can all go somewhere together to get to know one another."

Surprised by her sister's offer, Adriana hedged, "Maybe another time."

Jennifer didn't seem happy, but she said, "You mean you're staying? Will you be all right?"

"I'm fine." Now that she knew she would be with Val again. "But you'll still take Irina home, won't you?"

Todd assured her, "No problem."

"Thank you." Adriana hugged her sister, then Irina, whispering in her friend's ear. "And you... remember your promise."

Heaving a dramatic sigh but no word of protest, Irina went off with Jennifer and Todd, but when she glanced back, her expression was troubled, reminding Adriana of her earlier warning. Then, sensing a presence behind her, she forgot about everything but him.

"Val," she whispered as she turned to face him, thrilled by the longing in his gaze that matched her own. "I was afraid you wouldn't come."

"I almost did not."

"You could have joined us, you know. None of this would have been possible without your help."

"I was content watching from a distance."

She knew he meant that he'd been watching her. Her spirits soared and her heartbeat quickened. No man had ever made her feel so desirable.

Stepping closer, he frowned and inhaled deeply, his gaze settling on the rose in her hand. "The flower," he said. "Would you mind?"

"You want me to get rid of it? Are you allergic or something?"

"Yes, allergic," he agreed.

Thinking it was a shame—she'd thought to keep the rose in Eddie's memory—she set the flower down on an undecorated grave.

"You look lovely, as usual," Val said, his eyes sliding over her, warming her. "Though white is not the ordinary color for a funeral."

"Irina said Gypsies wear white as the color of mourning." Not to mention that she'd intentionally chosen something different than her usual deep jewel tones tonight. "And angels usually wear white. I like to imagine they'll come to carry Eddie away."

"I am sure they will. His soul was fairly innocent," he said, sounding as if he knew.

"You could sense that, huh?" she said as they walked along, skirting graves that sometimes dated back to the past century.

Speaking of angels, many stood poised on the old monuments, some life-size with wings unfurled and delicate arms reaching toward heaven. Even the vandals who'd chipped off noses and fingers through the years hadn't diminished the statues' power.

An unreadable expression on his face, Val eyed the pale figures as they passed by. While Adriana glanced back at the workers, who had shovels in hand.

"It's best not to think about it."

"How can I not? It's tragic that he died so young."

"At least he'll be somewhere else now... hopefully, a better place than earth." He glanced over the tombstones surrounding them. "They all are. The people here have all been buried decently, have all had prayers said for their immortal souls. They are at peace."

Such a curious statement, such a somber tone, as if he were deeply religious and in a very conservative way.

"So you don't think anybody here had to go to purgatory, huh?" They were in a Catholic cemetery, after all.

He gazed at her for a moment, then shrugged. "I would rather not think about purgatory...or hell. There is enough hell on earth—terrible things, more savage situations than any of these people ever dealt with in their lives."

She couldn't agree. "Some of these men could have been killed in war."

He nodded, remaining solemn. "War. I know it very well."

She wasn't certain what he could have been involved in personally, being thirty-seven or -eight at the most, but she said, "I guess Hungary hasn't had a very peaceful history."

"It has been invaded, overrun, so many times, it is difficult to keep count. Villages trembled before the likes of Mongol hordes, Turkish armies . . . who had no mercy, anyway." He had a faraway look, as if he were focusing on a vivid scene within. "People tried to take shelter from the mailed warriors who would cut their heads off with scimitars and build mountains of skulls."

"Yuck!"

Paying no attention to her expression of distaste, he went on, his voice full of dark emotion. "Even churches offered no asylum. Women, little children, old men, were dragged from behind altars. The strong and the comely were taken as slaves—the rest were tortured and killed. There was no one left to bury the bodies or to pray or to mourn. In my domain, that is why we deemed the most desperate of measures to be necessary. . . ."

They had come to the gate leading out of the graveyard and Val paused, glancing around at his surroundings, then at Adriana as if he'd suddenly become aware of where they really were and that she still walked beside him.

While she was now caught up by the history he'd been relating so passionately that it sounded as if he could have lived in another time—the Middle Ages, perhaps, or the fifteenth century. "The most desperate of measures? What do you mean?"

He took her hand. "Let us go somewhere else, do something more interesting."

"You're not going to answer my question?"

"It is not important. I was only talking."

Adriana started to object when she noticed Val's clenched jaw. The man was really tense. She wasn't certain how they'd progressed to such a strange topic to begin with, but she decided he must have studied a lot of history, perhaps at some university.

"So what can we do that will be more interesting?"

"Do you still want to accompany me on a photographic shoot?" Though his eyes and the way he held her hand said that he'd prefer more personal activities. "You could use some distraction."

Distraction. If anyone could offer that, Val could. Heat radiated up her arm and her pulse did a jig. "I'd love to see you at work." For the first time, she noticed he'd slung a camera strap over one shoulder.

"Then come."

They turned onto Broadway, which looked the same as it had the night before. Only the people were different. Val gave Adriana's hand a squeeze, then let go to retrieve his camera. Without his touch, she felt bereft. Looking around, she was also a bit uneasy, though she told herself that, no matter what happened, Val was there.

"So what do you plan to shoot?" she asked.

"Whatever the night brings me."

Brawlers . . . drug dealers . . . prostitutes? That's primarily what he would find of interest on this strip at night. For some reason, those kinds of people held little fascination for her.

"The night has its positive aspects, too," she told Val as he adjusted his camera's lens. "I mean, beyond sparkly city lights and great entertainment. Did you know most babies are born at night?"

He clicked off several shots of two scared-looking youths hurrying down the street, heads down, hands stuffed in their pockets.

"And most people die then, too," he countered absently.

Back to death. She shivered. They might have a love of the night in common, but Val's outlook on life in general was far darker than hers. The scene with the taxi replayed itself in her mind, not to mention those few moments when he had threatened to become violent.

What had happened to a man of apparent wealth and culture to make him attracted not only to the night, but to the seamier side of life?

Just when she was wondering what she was doing with this man she hardly knew instead of having returned home with her sister, Val wrapped an arm around her shoulders, reminding her. They were connected in some deep, mysterious way. His very touch made something inside her flower.

And his intense expression—the blatant need she recognized...knowing that need was for her—took her very breath away.

She leaned into him, rested her head against his shoulder as they strolled down Broadway. Suddenly the street seemed less forbidding. More intriguing. She relaxed and trusted that he would keep her safe.

Every so often they would stop and he would snap a few more photos of the denizens of the night.

Whether or not he did, she noticed the day people out of their element, too. An exhausted-looking woman in a professional dress carrying bags of groceries. A couple of teenagers in school uniforms playing tag on the street and laughing as if they didn't have a care in the world. A businessman coming from the elevated carrying a briefcase in one hand, a bunch of flowers in the other.

Adriana remembered all the renovated buildings she'd spotted on her way to Val's the day before. While it had its drawbacks, the neighborhood obviously wasn't as dangerous as she'd come to believe.

Lulled into a sense of security, Adriana was shaken when, less than a quarter of a block before them, a man charged out of an alley near the long-deserted Uptown Theater. He was hauling behind him a young blonde in a spangled jacket, short shorts and high heels. She was digging those heels into the pavement, resisting for all she was worth.

Homely face a mask of fury, the man stopped, turned and yelled, "When are you gonna learn you gotta pay for your keep, you little bitch?"

"Not tonight, please, Jack," she begged, tears streaming down her painted face. "I don't feel so good. Can't I skip even one night?"

"Don't give me no grief, Lilly!"

Adriana was appalled. The man was obviously a pimp, the girl his prostitute. And she *was* just a girl. Beneath the layers of makeup and masses of gelled blond hair, her face revealed her true youth.

Adriana grabbed on to Val's arm. "She can't be more than fifteen or sixteen. What in the world is she doing on the street?"

"Surviving."

"But that's awful."

She realized Val was too busy lining up shots of the tableau to be properly outraged. Lilly was struggling, trying to free herself from Jack. The pimp raised his arm and backhanded her hard across the face. Her head snapped back and she muffled a scream.

Drawing closer fast, Adriana yelled, "Hey! Stop that."

Jack turned a mean frown on her. "Mind your own business, lady, unless you want some of the same." He flexed his narrow shoulders under what looked like a lime green jacket beneath the streetlights.

"I'm okay, really," the girl squeaked, wiping at her tears with the back of a shaky hand.

Up close, she looked even younger, and Adriana wasn't about to walk away from the situation. Heart pounding, she raised her chin and gave the pimp her blackest stare.

Adriana warned him, "If you don't let go of her—"

"You'll what?"

"Call the police, for one!"

Laughing, the pimp let go of the girl, who was now sobbing openly. "That better, lady?" He advanced on Adriana, fist raised.

His mistake.

Before he could carry out his physical threat, Val stepped between them. With a deep-throated roar, he picked up the pimp by his scrawny neck, shook him like a rag doll and threw him into the alley so hard the man went flying back into a Dumpster that was overflowing with garbage. His head snapped into the metal edge. He slid down to the filthy pavement, body lolling to one side, obviously unconscious.

"You shouldn't'a done that!" Lilly wailed. "Now I'll get the blame, and I don't want to be nowhere near Jack when he's really uptight!"

Lilly appeared so terrified that Adriana forgot to be afraid herself even though Val had shown his capacity for violence twice in as many days. Besides—having decked the pimp, Val had returned to his normal well-contained self. He wasn't even breathing hard. She wrapped her arms around the girl's thin body.

"Let's get out of here." She gave Val a beseeching look. "Maybe we could go somewhere nearby to calm her down? A coffee shop?"

He nodded. "On the next block."

Even as Adriana led the shaking girl away, she glanced back at the nasty Jack, who was still out for the count.

"Oh, God, what am I gonna do now?" Lilly moaned.

A few minutes later, they entered a greasy spoon that was empty but for a man sitting at the counter and muttering to himself over a bowl of soup. Once ensconced in a back table, they quickly gave the waitress their orders, Adriana insisting the girl eat despite her protests. Only then did she follow up on the girl's complaint.

"What do you want to do, Lilly," she probed, "now that Jack will be angry with you?"

The blonde fingered the distinctive gold cross she wore on a chain—a dove was etched at the junctures of the two stems. "I don't know what to do."

"You want to keep working for Jack?"

"No. I hate it." Tears pooled in her great blue eyes and fear pulled at her delicate features. "But I got nowhere else to go...and he's not all bad, anyhow. Found me at the bus station, gave me a place to stay."

"Bus station?" Val echoed, his gaze centered on the cross she still toyed with. "You are from another city?"

"A small town not too far from Kenosha. Um, that's Wisconsin." Lilly stared at the sunglasses he'd slipped on.

"You ran away from your parents?"

"I was having some trouble at home." She gulped. "Now I wish I'd never left."

"Then maybe you should go back," Adriana suggested.

"Can't. Besides, my mom will be really mad at me."

"Are you sure she's not worrying about you?"

"Maybe. Yeah, I guess."

"How old are you?" Val asked.

Lilly hesitated. "Jack told me to say eighteen." She chewed at her lower lip. "I guess it won't hurt nothing—I'll be fifteen next month."

Adriana swallowed hard. She couldn't imagine herself on her own at that age. Surely Lilly didn't have to be, either. "Don't you think your mom would like you to come home?"

Lilly shrugged and her full lower lip trembled. "Don't matter what I think. I don't have no money, anyhow. Jack keeps it for me. Says that way it's safe—only he tells me how to spend it. He wouldn't like me going home. And my mom sure don't have nothing. My dad spends every extra penny on booze."

Undoubtedly the reason the girl ran away in the first place. Adriana took a deep breath. Sending her home didn't sound like the perfect solution to her problems . . . but it sure sounded a lot better than her walking the streets and letting a sleaze like Jack control her. At least she'd have a chance.

Val seemed to think so, as well, for he produced his wallet and pulled out another hundred-dollar bill. "Will this be enough to buy your fare to Kenosha?"

A hopeful glimmer in her eyes, Lilly looked from Val to Adriana. "Sure. That's plenty for a ticket—too late to leave tonight, but first bus out is five in the morning." She sounded as if she'd memorized the schedule, as if she'd been thinking about going home for a while. "So that's enough time for both of you, right? Just, please, don't make me do nothing really gross."

"Make you . . ." Adriana started as she comprehended the girl's meaning.

"We don't expect anything of you," Val assured her. "Consider this a gift from someone older and wiser."

"You're kidding, right?"

"I do not kid."

But he certainly dazzled. Again, he was helping out someone he didn't even know. Adriana couldn't stop staring at him. Val turned to face her and, for a moment, they were alone, someplace where no one could bring her down.

Then the waitress came with their food and brought her straight back to reality.

Once again, Val pulled out the small pouch and laced his extra-rare steak with herbs. Lilly seemed curious, but she was too busy stuffing her mouth with food to comment. Wondering if that damned pimp starved the poor kid when she was making his living for him, Adriana found she was hungry, as well.

A half hour passed before they left the greasy spoon. Once on the street, Val searched the area with his intense gaze as if he had special antennae.

"The scum is gone," he stated, obviously meaning Jack.

"Good!" Lilly said, sounding relieved. She fingered her cross and stared down at her toes. "Um, I don't know how to thank you."

"You will thank me by going straight downtown to the bus station and waiting there until the Kenosha bus leaves in the morning," Val said seriously. "No more making friends with strangers."

"But you're a stranger. Both of you." Shyly, Lilly hugged Adriana, then tried to do the same to Val.

He jumped back as if burned. "A handshake will suffice," he said stiffly.

A bit downcast at the rejection, Lilly nevertheless complied. But when Val offered to flag down a taxi for her, she laughed and told him she was more comfortable on public transportation. They waited with her until the next bus arrived and watched her safely alight. She paid the driver, then rushed to the nearest window, where she pressed her nose against the glass and waved at them.

Lilly really was just a kid.

And Adriana glowed with happiness that Val had gotten her off the streets. So when he asked, "Where to?" she quickly answered, "Your place." Caution shadowed his features, and Adriana thought he was about to refuse. She moved closer and purred, "Please?"

"I should take you home."

Her pulse rushed through her at his very closeness. "But you won't if I ask you not to."

"No."

"I don't want to be alone." She took off his sunglasses and slipped them into his breast pocket. Stared longingly into his shadowed golden eyes. "I want to be with you." Adriana was surprised that she meant that in every sense of the word.

"I only hope you do not regret that wish."

Despite the doubts she'd had about Val, her instincts told her he was a man who would never hurt her... a man she could trust with her life.

Miklos Rakosi waited in the shadows of the doorway as Kadar and his new woman strolled past him, so intent on each other that they saw nothing else.

Rakosi had returned to the Gold Coast neighborhood where he'd first seen them together, had asked around and found out where Adriana Thorn worked. She was a deejay at After Dark. She'd also been a friend of the victim. He'd followed Kadar at a distance since the moment he'd left the house and had seen her at the cemetery.

He'd been shadowing them since, had seen the altercation with the little whore, had heard their conversation as they said their goodbyes.

What a waste.

Rakosi chuckled and left the doorway. Kadar and the Thorn woman were crossing the street. His nemesis would be livid if he knew his enemy had been so very, very close....

And Kadar would have sensed his presence had he not been wearing the medallion. He fingered the token that gave him some of the power Kadar himself enjoyed. Rakosi had always been resentful that he had not been able to employ those powers on his own. Damn his father for taking up with such a weak-spirited woman as his mother!

The Thorn woman—he intended to get to her. But first, he had other fish to fry. With a grin, Rakosi took off in the opposite direction.

Kadar couldn't win. In the end, he would be finished by his own disease.

CHAPTER SEVEN

Val knew Adriana desired him every bit as much as he desired her. Her request to be taken to his home had surprised him, however, and he had agreed before he'd thought the thing through. He knew she hadn't longed to come here just to talk . . . and anything else would be dangerous for both of them.

So what in the world was he doing?

Telling himself he was a fool, he held open the front door to the unlit cavern that was his home for a time. "Step inside, but be careful until I provide us with some light."

"It's so dark in here," Adriana murmured, sliding by him too closely for his own comfort. "Doesn't your chandelier work?"

"I have not felt the need to try it."

Val closed the door, cutting off the streetlight but for the glow through the unboarded front windows. Darkness surrounded them where they stood. Darkness in which he could lose himself with her. She shifted, stirring the air, teasing him with the scent of her essence and a subtle perfume that hinted of lilacs in bloom. Her breath quickened slightly and he knew she felt the instant attraction of their closeness.

"Candles suit me. Wait here a moment."

His night vision was far better than hers. While he walked straight to the fireplace without mishap, she would probably stumble over something.

He picked up the matches from the mantel and lit the candles, first there, then around the rest of the room. Meanwhile, she wandered inside, dreamily unbuttoning and removing her outer garment, casting it onto the sofa.

Her white dress glowed against the shadows of the room and enticingly swirled around her slim body. The material was fine, translucent. The bodice was cut deep and wide, showing off her creamy shoulders, the slight swell of her breasts and the length of her graceful neck to advantage. The mere thought of tasting that expanse of skin set him afire inside.

But if he thought Adriana would throw herself into his arms and beg him to make love to her the moment they had some privacy, he was mistaken. She stayed a distance away, her body language and facial expressions showing her inner turmoil—that she both wanted and was a bit afraid of him.

As well she should be.

Hoping to relax her, he turned on the radio to a classical station and asked, "Would you like some wine?"

"Sounds wonderful."

Adriana seemed relieved, as if he'd given her a reprieve. Perhaps she would change her mind about what she wanted of him, after all.

He would try not to be too disappointed.

From a cabinet with leaded-glass doors built into a wall, he removed two crystal goblets and a decanter of his favorite merlot. "I hope you like red."

"Very much."

He set the glasses on the end table and, turning on the lamp, decanted the wine, fascinated as always by the deep red rivulet that pooled at the bottom of the crystal. Then he held out a glass, catching a glimpse of her exotic loveliness through the crystal goblet. The wine sloshed a bit as she took it, making it appear as if she were enveloped in blood.

Heart pounding, breath sharp, he ripped his gaze away and controlled his imagination. "A toast?"

"To the beginning of a very unusual, very intense relationship," she said.

Adriana had no idea of how right she was. Val clinked his crystal to hers and savored a sip of the merlot at the same time she did. Even so, he was intrigued, watching the muscles of her throat delicately work as she swallowed. Her responding smile dazzled him, and he gazed hungrily at her full mouth, wanting to sip the wine from her lips.

"This is a strange place for you to be living," she said, startling him into a change of thought.

"Strange?" he echoed.

"It's so old and needs so much work."

She was staring at the intricately carved wood of the mantelpiece. To make it shine once again, multiple layers of dirt and varnish and stain would have to be removed. No easy task, he was certain.

He swirled the liquid in his glass, warming it between his hands. "My family's estate in Hungary is much, much older, and repairs far greater than those required here are a constant headache, so I feel very much at home."

"Then you're going to work on this place? I mean, you own it, right?"

"Of course." A landlord could walk in unannounced and surprise him. He couldn't have that. To please her, he said, "I have had thoughts about how I might renovate."

"It does have great potential," she admitted. "How did you find this particular house, anyway?"

Thinking that she must be using her questions as a delaying tactic, he played along with her. "I had my agent contact a local Realtor. The house was mine before I ever arrived in Chicago."

"Then you mean to stay?"

Her voice quivered slightly, as if she were afraid he might deny it. He only wished he could tell her what she wanted to hear.

"For a while, until my work here is done," he said.

She frowned at that. "Your photography?"

"And other interests."

"Oh, yes, some business with a relative, wasn't it?"

"Exactly."

"What kind of business? If you don't mind my asking."

It wouldn't hurt to tell her, "I am to retrieve a family heirloom."

"That's it?" She definitely sounded disappointed. "And then you'll be leaving?"

"Perhaps. If I have no other reason to stay."

Adriana could convince him to stay, Val thought...at least for a while. Though his family was in Hungary, he had no companion who awaited him. No soul mate. He'd never found one. And not for the lack of trying.

"So when you do leave," Adriana was saying, "what will you do with the house?"

"I haven't thought that far ahead."

"Oh."

Her inquisitiveness winding down, Adriana seemed a bit melancholy. She sipped at her wine again, and this time a drop splashed on her breast, the ruby red glaring against the stark white material of her dress. He grew taut with his desire to explore that territory, to taste the wine from something other than his glass.

To make love to her, no matter the consequences.

She claimed to have chosen to wear white as an alternative color of mourning. And as a reflection of her faith in an afterworld. He only wished he could stop thinking of her as a very lovely sacrificial victim....

Val continued staring at the wine staining her bodice. He was mesmerized by it. Mesmerized by her. It had been so long since he'd taken a woman...and he wasn't certain that he'd ever been as taken himself as he was with Adriana Thorn. He wouldn't be able to resist seizing what he was certain she was subtly offering. But he had to be careful that he didn't let things go too far, let her know who he really was.

Concentrating, he barely heard her next question.

"I'm so fascinated by this place. Are you willing to show me the upstairs...your bedroom?"

His bedroom. All senses alert, Val stared at her, meeting wide, willing gray eyes.

He couldn't stand it. He couldn't refuse her.

Emptying his glass, he set it down on the mantel and picked up one of the candles. Then, pulse pounding through his veins, he held out his hand, "Come with me."

Lips trembling, she put her hand in his and allowed him to lead her up the stairs.

The candle Val was carrying pooled light across the stairs as they ascended. Imagination working overtime, Adriana felt as if she were being led to a secret chamber in an old Gothic novel. Nerves. Hers were jumping. They both knew why she'd asked Val to take her to his home. But now she was having second thoughts, analyzing her motivations, wondering if she was desperate to get closer to him as some kind of denial of death.

Val wasn't rushing to prove anything, and for that she was thankful. His consideration gave her time to breathe. To think. Her major reflection being, why was she so bereft every time she thought of him picking up and leaving town?

One would imagine he'd put her under some kind of magic spell. Even now, she felt as if she were operating half in this world, half in a dream. A state that was becoming more and more familiar to her.

While Val's touch was cool, heat spread up her arm to make her entire body glow with warmth. And the deep longing she'd felt off and on since meeting him surfaced.

"This way," he said, turning to the right at the landing, the timbre of his voice penetrating her very being.

They approached a door, and she assumed his bedroom lay on the other side. Her breath quickened. All kinds of imaginings whirled through her head. Exciting. So very exciting. And equally scary.

So when he opened the door and invited her in, she hesitated just a moment. But if she didn't accept, she would never know what might lie on the other side. What they might mean to each other.

Again, as he had when they'd entered the house, Val said, "Wait there while I see to some light."

And the fact that he didn't mean electric lamps seemed the most normal thing in the world. She watched him move around, touching flame to myriad white candles of all thicknesses and heights.

Soon she could see well enough to determine his private quarters were more fully furnished than any room she'd explored so far, as if he spent the most time here. All the pieces were antiques in prime condition. A dresser with intricate brass knobs. A chest of drawers. A chaise longue. An armoire. A four-poster bed with heavy wine red hangings that could be closed to shut out anything from disturbing the occupants inside.

Thinking about being cocooned with Val started her heart pounding. She lowered her gaze to the mattress... and widened her eyes at the sight that greeted her.

"Valentin?"

"Yes?" he asked without turning from the candle he was lighting.

"We have company."

A sleepy-eyed black dog—a scruffy Lab mix—lay curled in the middle of the wine red coverlet. When Val approached, the animal raised its ears, one of which had been recently battered, and sat up. All the while the dog whined through its nose and wagged its matted tail.

"I thought we had this discussion before," Val said sternly, gazing into the dog's big brown eyes, "and decided you were not to make yourself at home up here."

Appearing dejected, ears and tail suddenly droopy, the dog slipped off the bed, dropping to the floor.

"Try to remember that your bed is downstairs," he told the dog, giving it an encouraging pat that raised its ears and made its tail wag. "And your food. Go on now."

Eyebrows arched at the scenario, Adriana said, "I didn't know you had a dog."

"I don't."

Like he didn't have cats, either. "Then what do you call that?" she asked as the animal left the room, limping slightly.

"He was hurt," Val said, sounding almost defensive. "I merely gave him temporary respite from the vagaries of the world."

Adriana grinned. So Val had a dog. She wondered how the cats liked the newest addition to the household. She chose not to ask. Why push it? Val wanted to believe that he was unencumbered, that he could pick up and take off for Hungary anytime he wanted, but he simply had too many creatures depending on him. Subconsciously, he must want to stay. Eventually, he would come to terms with the fact.

In the meantime, any doubts she'd had about being here with him melted away. Terrible temper or not, this was a man who gave a helping hand freely to others, whether human or beast. As for his not having an aura, being involved in black magic...Irina was going off the deep end with her attachment to anything metaphysical, Adriana decided.

For, knowing the little she did about him, how could she distrust Val?

The longing grew stronger.

And in this room where time was suspended, being with Val more intimately seemed so right. She couldn't think of anything else. He stood at the edge of the bed, barely a yard from her. She drew closer to him, taking in every detail of his face beneath the thick black hair that strayed across his forehead—high Magyar cheekbones, straight nose and a wide mouth that at times could be cruel, but at the moment was utterly sensual.

As were the golden brown eyes driving into her, trying to read her thoughts.

"Like what you see?" she whispered, stopping a heartbeat away from him.

"More than you can imagine."

"Don't be too sure." Her pulse rushed through her. "I have a great imagination."

Right now she was envisioning what it would be like to be surrounded by him...

And as if he were actually inside her head, Val slid his palms over her arms. Her flesh responded, pebbling even when his hands continued on, his arms eventually encircling her back. His golden eyes slitted. Her breath caught in her throat. Then he was helping her—his mouth covering hers, he was breathing for her.

"Val," she murmured.

Adriana.

Without speaking, he called her name and she heard.

The longing deepened, her mind becoming thick and fuzzy with her building desire. She'd never felt like this before. Not about anyone. She couldn't define the thing that consumed her, the need that went beyond her experience. She only knew that Val was the one who could help her assuage it.

Suddenly he ended the kiss, whipped his head away and shoved her from him, his fingers digging into the soft flesh of her upper arms.

"You are free to change your mind," he told her.

"I don't want to change my mind." She wanted to be cocooned in the four-poster, Val taking her to heights of ecstasy she'd only dreamed of before.

"You must be sure... Must change your mind now if you will... or I do not think I can stop."

She lost herself to his gaze. "Then don't."

His arms moved around her again, his mouth working magic. He kissed her lips, her nose, her chin. He laved her throat, lingering there for a moment before moving lower. Her breasts strained through the thin material of her dress; his teeth teased them until the nipples hardened into sensitive peaks. Pressing her to him, he lifted her skirt, and with his free hand explored the exposed flesh above the sheer stockings held up by a lacy garter belt.

Val's hand on the inside of her thighs made Adriana quake inside. He set to examining the simple maze of her undergarments, found and breeched the edge of the lace covering her. She moaned and pushed forward until he easily insinuated a single finger into her heated center. Her knees weakened and she clung to him, her back and neck arching, her long hair streaming free behind her as he moved his hand, plundering her with sensation.

His mouth connected with her throat. He worked his magic there as he ripped away the restricting lace below and allowed the undergarment to drop to the floor. Again he found her wet warmth, and she raised a leg, curling it around his thigh and knee so she would be more open to his pleasuring her. Rocking against his hand, she made soft, whimpering sounds as the pressure inside her built. But, through a sensual haze, wondering why he didn't stop so they could both undress.

"Open your eyes," Val commanded in that hypnotic tone. "I want to see your pleasure."

Panting now, she forced her lids slowly open as he increased the tempo of his hand. "What about your pleasure?"

"No need to rush," he answered. "Besides, you are very pleasing, indeed."

His words allowed her to give over to the demand he created. But a minute more and she was crying out, the sound coming from somewhere deep inside her.

With a triumphant growl, Val removed his fingers from her heated flesh and used them to unzip the back of her dress. Consumed by the dizzying force he'd brought forth in her, she was of little help. The dress dropped to her ankles, and she stood before him clad in nothing but a lace-edged camisole, the matching garter belt, stockings and shoes.

He lay her back against the bed and removed her shoes, letting them slip to the floor unheeded. And when she gripped the edge of the camisole, he said, "No. Leave it on. Let me imagine your full beauty a while longer."

Obeying, she relaxed as best she could, watched him do a male striptease. His golden eyes were hot on her as he kicked off his own shoes while slowly removing his jacket and shirt. She noted his chest and shoulders and upper arms were firmly muscled, his waist tight and trim. He dropped the trousers, and her gaze lowered to where he strained against his briefs. Then they, too, were discarded, and he stood before her nude and definitely ready to take his pleasure.

Once more, she tried removing the camisole, once more he dissuaded her, this time physically. Climbing onto the bed, he inserted himself between her knees and caught her wrists with his hands. His fingers felt like iron manacles as he pulled her hands over her head.

"Open for me," he commanded softly, and she spread her legs wider.

Without any preliminaries, without the use of his hands to guide himself, he unerringly found her, impaled her so swiftly that her back arched and she pushed at him in response.

"You are so smooth, so welcoming. No wonder I could not resist your invitation."

And she had invited. Had been waiting for this nearly since the moment they'd met. Him inside her, thrusting harder. Her lifting her hips, wrapping first one leg, then the other, around his back, so as to give him complete access. With each stroke her excitement rose so that she grew restless. Needing. Wanting.

He suckled her breasts through the satin and lace, the garment's texture increasing the excitement of his mouth. Then, with a nip that left her gasping, he allowed his mouth to wander higher, over the swell of her breasts, up the expanse along her collarbone and around to her jaw. He suckled the flesh directly below her left ear.

She throbbed all over. Inside and out. She arched her neck, crying, "More. Please, more!" Not even knowing exactly what more she wanted.

With a groan, he complied, thrusting faster inside her, sucking harder on the sensitive flesh beneath her ear. Her heart pumped, her pulse raced. She turned inside out with wanting, was teetering at the pinnacle, and still she knew she could climb higher.

"Do it! Do it now!" she demanded hoarsely, pressing her neck harder into his mouth.

Val's body tensed and he bit down on her flesh. Tiny pricks of pain pushed her over the phantom edge. Blood flowed through her at a quickening speed as she cried out. This time the pleasure was multiplied. She was reeling. Floating. Unable to speak...

And Val released a roar that made her tremble inside. Was that ecstasy she heard?

Or agony?

His magic wreaked havoc with her senses even after they collapsed into each other's arms. Everything seemed unreal. And wonderful, if a little distant. Her vision was blurred. Her concentration negligible. She was content merely to exist, to float forever.

The myriad candles set around the room seemed to multiply, making the room seem enchanted. Definitely romantic. And undeniably erotic.

Sometime later, she stretched and spoke as if in a dream. "I never realized it would be like this between us."

And Val rolled over, scooping her to his side. "You have no idea of what it really might be like."

She thought to question that curious statement issued in such a serious tone, but she couldn't summon the energy. Her body felt so light, as if she could rise and leave it behind. Or, perhaps, float in truth. Fly. She'd had tons of dreams of flying as a child—probably true of most everyone—but hers had never quite gone away.

Smiling, she snuggled closer to Val, seeking his warmth, but his flesh wasn't heated and sweaty as hers still was. His skin was dry and barely warm to the touch. She was surprised that he'd cooled off so fast.

Her neck throbbed where he'd nipped her and she set the flesh against that of his chest and listened to his heartbeat. Mesmerizing.

Realizing she wasn't exactly coherent, Adriana gave it up and let her mind drift, suspecting that, despite the fires that still burned deep inside her, despite the intense feelings she wanted to share with Val, she was having a difficult time keeping her eyes open.

She focused on Val's handsome, enigmatic features, wanting them to be the last thing she saw before she slept and the first thing she saw when she awakened.

Adriana woke, muzzy and disoriented, restless after having an intense erotic dream. Or was it? She remembered asking Val to take her to his home, remembered him leading her up the stairs to his bedroom, remembered . . .

"Val?" she murmured, but received no response.

She stretched out, searching the bed with a lazy hand. Empty. Eyes adjusting to the first gray preceding daybreak, she realized she was in her own room, her own bed.

But how had she gotten there?

She sat up, concentrated. Remembered making love. More than once.

Or had she been in the thrall of erotic dreams all night long? Val certainly wasn't around, though her body told her he had been. . . .

And where was her beloved cat, who always slept with her, if not on her?

"Phantom?" she called, but heard no responding meow. Through bleary eyes, she searched the room until she spotted the black ball of fur tucked into a corner. She stumbled out of bed. "There you are."

Then she stopped short when the wide-eyed cat fluffed herself up and growled deep in her throat.

Concerned, never having seen Phantom acting anything but loving toward her, Adriana stooped and held out her hand.

"Honey, what's wrong?" she murmured soothingly. "Aren't you feeling well?" She wasn't feeling so well herself, but she tried not to panic, thinking the cat might be sick. "C'mon here, Phantom."

The quizzical lightning-split face tilted and the cat stared at her suspiciously, sniffing the air as if her mistress were a stranger.

"Hey, sweetie girl, it's me. C'mon," Adriana urged her. "C'mon."

Making up her mind, the cat carefully inched forward and, as if realizing that this was, indeed, the mistress she loved, finally relaxed and rubbed against the extended hand. Adriana smoothed down the fur along her spine, and Phantom responded as always. She wasn't hurt. Her nose was cool and wet. And her purr-box was working perfectly well. She was vibrating like an engine.

Relieving Adriana greatly.

So what had all that silliness been about? Then it hit her. Phantom must have been put off by Val's scent on her...and, more unusual, the scent of their lovemaking. She hadn't been with a man since finding the cat, so this was new and maybe scary to the animal.

Maybe Phantom was simply jealous.

Picking her up, she squeezed and kissed the silly furball. "Don't scare me like that."

The faint smell of coffee tempted her and she knew Jennifer would be up having breakfast, getting ready to leave for work. Deciding she would surprise her sister and join her, Adriana set down the cat and rose, swaying with the abrupt movement. What in the world? Surely she wasn't coming down with the flu or something. Her world righted and she realized she was stark naked.

She found a robe and drew it around her, wondering why everything that happened after entering Val's bedroom the night before was one big blur, a confusion of vague images and memories.

Wonderful, scintillating visions.

She might think their lovemaking really had been one long series of dreams if her body didn't feel so thoroughly and deliciously ravished. Not one inch of her flesh had been neglected. And every inch longed to be touched again. She sighed.

Then vague memories floated through her mind. Val helping her to dress...bringing her out to a waiting taxi...seeing her to the elevator and to her door in the middle of the night. Curious that she didn't remember the security guard Henry saying anything to them. Could he have not noticed or had she forgotten?

Adriana hadn't any more of a clue than she did as to the time she'd arrived home.

A glance in the mirror brought her back to the present. Her hair looked like a fright wig. Adriana picked through the long strands, untangling the knots, then found a brush and worked on it till the wavy strands shone. She gathered the heavy mass behind her, thinking to clip it back, then noticed the marking on the left side of her neck.

Though the room was still shadowed in the gray predawn light, a closer inspection in the mirror revealed a slight bruising...and were those breaks in the skin?

Her pulse began to thrum.

She dropped her hair and stepped back from the mirror, frowning. She vaguely remembered urging Val to do something...then feeling him bite her.

A bit embarrassed that she'd gotten so carried away in the throes of passion, Adriana thought she'd rather be discreet than give Jennifer reason to make comment. To that end, she drew her hair forward, brushing it neatly over her shoulders, so that it hid the evidence of her and Val's intensity.

Thoughts of Val and their night together trailing after her, Adriana left the bedroom, blinking against the sudden intrusion of lights that had been turned on throughout the apartment. Her eyes felt raw. But, rather than coming down with something, she was probably just exhausted.

When she hit the kitchen, Jennifer was using the remote control to turn on the television mounted below the cabinets, undoubtedly to catch the morning stock averages.

Her sister gave her a shocked expression and instantly muted the sound. "You're up after getting home so late?"

"How late?" Adriana asked casually, pouring herself a cup of coffee.

"You don't even know what time you got home?"

"Maybe I just want to know if you were waiting up for me, *Mom,*" she said in a teasing tone, though her not remembering bugged her.

But Jennifer wasn't offering any answers. "Oh, dear, I do sound like Mom, don't I?"

"Sometimes. But that's okay."

Adriana kissed her sister on the cheek and threw herself in the chair opposite, stealing a piece of toast. As usual, Jennifer had risen, showered, dressed and made herself breakfast—all before dawn. She would be leaving for work as the sun rose over Lake Michigan, often the time Adriana returned home if she went out after work.

Jennifer used the remote to turn up the sound on the television. Adriana noticed the woman newscaster's serious expression.

"Just in. Another violent death mars Chicago's streets, this time at the Fleetways bus station just west of the Loop."

Adriana was startled. Bus station?

"How cheerful," Jennifer muttered.

"The body was found at four-thirty, approximately one hour after the murder."

Jennifer went for the remote as if to change channels. Pulse jolting, Adriana put her hand over her sister's, stopping her. "I want to hear this."

"The victim was a young woman, whom the police suspect to be a minor, though no identification was found with the body."

Wanting to deny what she was thinking, Adriana felt sick inside.

"She was blond and blue-eyed, wearing short shorts and a spangled jacket."

She felt as if someone had punched her in the stomach. It couldn't be... She prayed she was wrong as the newscast ran live footage of the body bag being hoisted into the ambulance.

"A piece of jewelry was found near the girl's body. The chain was broken, assumably in the struggle. Still attached to the chain was a cross engraved with a dove."

Adriana was mesmerized by the shot of an evidence technician wearing gloves dropping an etched cross into a small plastic bag. In her mind, she saw Lilly fiddling with that same cross. No ID, no photo, but in her heart, she knew Lilly was dead.

"The police fear a serial killer is on the loose. As it was from the first victim only days ago, the girl's blood was completely drained from her body—"

"Omigod!" Jennifer whispered. "Just like your friend, Eddie."

Tasting the bile rising to rip at her throat, Adriana pushed herself from the table, muttering, "Excuse me."

"Hey, are you all right?" Jennifer called after her.

Adriana didn't answer but flew to her room and the toilet, where she threw up.

Afterward, she lay back against the tile wall, her head spinning, sick with guilt. She had no doubts that Lilly was the second victim. And if she and Val hadn't talked the girl into going home, and therefore waiting at the bus station—the wrong place at the wrong time—Lilly would still be alive.

A knock at the bathroom door startled her. "Adriana?"

She bolted away from the door and toward the bathtub. "I'm fine, Jens. I was just upset."

She was still upset, didn't know if she would ever feel okay again.

"You want to talk about it?"

Talk about her and Val being amongst the last people to see the girl alive? Like Eddie?

"No. I'm going to take a shower. That'll make me feel better." She turned on the water. "You go ahead to work."

"If you're sure."

"Positive."

But no shower would ever make her feel better after sending a kid off to her death.

Weird. Two identical murders, and she and Val had been among the last to see each of those victims alive. Them and the murderer.

What if...

She pictured Val, having given Eddie a hundred-dollar bill, Lilly the same. There was no connection, she told herself. There wasn't! It was a coincidence.

If only she could remember exactly what happened the night before.

If only she hadn't had that wine.

If only...

All the *if onlys* in the world wouldn't bring Lilly back.

Adriana was not only sick with guilt... but with suspicion. The similarities in the two cases were too great to be mere coincidence. So what did that mean? It couldn't be Val, she told herself. After they'd sent Lilly on her way, they'd been together.

Until when? What time had he brought her home? Hard as she tried, she couldn't remember.

What if Val had left her here before three-thirty—the reported time of the girl's death?

"The visitor no one invited to the party. The stalker in the alley with unblinking eyes...who waits patiently through a lifetime. But in the end, always pounces.

"A stranger who follows us down city streets, hiding in doorways, slinking into shadows. In fear, we glance behind us, always trying to stay one step ahead.

"But we do not really wish to see. We do not hear.

"We do not believe.

"Inescapable. Unrelenting. An escort for the journey on a subway train hurtling toward destiny. We arrive at an unknown station too soon.

"We argue. We fight. We lose.

"Death...

"A fierce figure in the underground parking lot waiting by the door. It opens.

"To darkness?

"The next world?

"Either. Both. Have no fear. Night possesses its own eternal beauty.

"Even darkness lives."

Heaving a trembly sigh, Adriana finished her monologue, a eulogy to honor both Eddie and Lilly. Her audience probably thought the number that followed, a classical rock version of *Amazing Grace,* was an odd choice for a dance club, but no one complained.

She left her post, her mind still in turmoil. Wondering if Val would show tonight.

Distracted, she didn't see the man until she nearly ran smack into him. He gripped her arms tight. Her heart pounded. Her nerves shattered. In one instant, she wanted to introduce *him* to Death and see where it would take him.

"Hi ya, babe. Some monologue."

"Get your hands off me before I call a bouncer," she said coldly.

Stone Drake gave her the slow, crooked smile that she knew only too well. "At your service."

CHAPTER EIGHT

"You're working here?" Adriana didn't know whether to be more shocked or outraged. "Since when?"

"Frank Nieman hired me this afternoon." Stone assumed his lady-killer pose—the hooded dark eyes, the slouch, the lazy grin. "He needed somebody with confidence and muscle."

Adriana wondered how she'd ever found him appealing. Stone might be attractive, but now that she knew his true nature, she realized his manner was studied, a little coarse. He was a con man, a charming sociopath with little, if any, conscience.

She said bitterly, "Yeah, you have muscles all right and no compunction about using them on people weaker than yourself."

"Aw, come on, babe." He leaned toward her, his smile tightening when she scowled. "You make it sound like I'm some woman beater. I never laid a hand on you or any other female."

"You don't have to use physical force to abuse a relationship."

"I never meant you any real harm. Let's let bygones be bygones."

"Bygones, bull, I'm going to talk to Frank."

"You want him to know I left you handcuffed to a bed?"

That stopped her cold. The reason why she hadn't told anyone but Jennifer about the incident. She'd been too embarrassed. What she'd assumed was a little creative love play had been Stone's way of keeping her from stopping him when he'd left with her things.

Nevertheless, she threatened, "I don't care what I have to admit to. I'm going to see that you're fired."

"Hey, Adriana, come on." He straightened and, to his credit, actually appeared contrite. "Look, I'm sorry. I needed the money... real bad. Otherwise I wouldn't have touched your things. I was in trouble."

"It's too late for apologies. And you're always in trouble." Though it had taken her a while to realize why—he worked only sporadically and what he made he invested in crazy schemes or gambled away. "You're a selfish pig if you think you can get away with stealing my equipment and all my savings. Not to mention that you left me helpless and vulnerable. I could have starved to death."

"But you didn't, did you? You're a real capable woman." The way he said it made her think he admired her. She softened just a tad until he added, "I knew you'd find a way to free yourself."

Only by taking the bed apart and dragging the headboard with her to a phone. "I want you out of here." She looked around. "Where's Frank?"

Stone tried to slide an arm about her shoulders, frowning when she shook him off. "Adriana, please, I need this gig. If I can keep it, I'll be able to return your mixes. You won't have to pay for them."

"Gee, thanks."

Ignoring her sarcasm, he said, "I know I've made some bad mistakes. But I'm gonna try to make up for them. I'll even promise to repay the money." Again, he attempted to reach out to her, but she slapped him away. "Hell, think about how good we were together. I only wish you could find it in your heart to take me back. I love you . . . I always have."

Unbelievable. But she'd believed it once.

About to say that no way on God's earth would she be so stupid a second time, she sighted Val suddenly emerging from the surrounding crowd. His dark glasses tucked in his jacket pocket, he turned the full blaze of his penetrating eyes on her.

She froze, caught her breath, a shiver of fear running up and down her spine.

Adriana truly appeared to be frightened. Even as he felt a twinge—he'd seen far too much terror in his life—Val couldn't help assuming an accusatory stance. How dare another man profess devotion to *his* woman?

He approached, knowing he had to keep his hands off the encroacher. He addressed Adriana, "And who is this?"

"Uh, Valentin Kadar, meet Stone Drake."

An ordinary wretch with a relatively good-looking face and a furtive gleam in his eyes.

Val didn't return Drake's smile. "The thief? The scoundrel who was so unkind to you, Adriana? I cannot say that this is a pleasure."

The other man's smile faded and he quickly turned away. "Guess you *have* been bad-mouthing me, haven't you?"

"I wouldn't call the truth bad-mouthing," she said.

"Would you like me to take this man outside? I can make him return what he stole from you."

His expression wary, Drake nevertheless puffed out his chest. "Hey, man, I'm the bouncer here."

While Adriana's eyes widened with apprehension. "Please." She made a placating gesture. "Don't hurt him, Val. I want my mixes back—but violence isn't necessary. And Stone actually does work here...at least for the moment."

Val's anger flared, along with a couple of bright flashes that erupted amid the throng near the dance floor. He scowled as Irina Murphy rushed away, a small camera in her hand.

"You protect this ingrate. Why? Do you still want him?"

Drake balled his fists. "Nobody has to protect me."

"Stop this right now!" Adriana stepped between the antagonists, pushed at Drake. "Mind your business, Stone. Go find some other customer to hassle."

Drake looked petulant. "Who is this guy, anyway? Your new boyfriend?"

"Uh, something like that." She pushed at Drake again. "So go away."

Stone Drake obviously had good survival instincts. Giving Val one last glance, he turned and stalked off.

Adriana's gaze was steady on him. "He's a con man and a thief, but he doesn't deserve to die."

"Die?" What was she talking about? "I had no intention of killing anyone." Though Val would have enjoyed threatening Drake, perhaps even roughing him up a bit. But the distance he sensed in Adriana herself was his major worry. She wasn't herself. "What's wrong?"

"Wrong?"

She blinked as bright pinpoints of light flashed in the dimness again, this time near the entrance to the bar. The little Gypsy was taking more photographs. Val gave Irina a filthy glance even as she scooted out of arm's length.

Adriana was the woman he wished to reach for. He placed a hand on her shoulder and felt her flesh shudder slightly. "You are distraught. You should be seeking comfort from me."

"I wish I could find comfort."

He supposed he could attempt to mesmerize her with his gaze, overwhelm her with the power of his persona, but he chose not to try. He wanted Adriana Thorn's true heart and soul. "Again, I ask you what is wrong."

"I have a lot of things on my mind."

"Like Stone Drake?" That was all that could have come between them since last they were together. "Would you really choose him over me?"

She made a face. "Of course not." But again she paused. "I—I just need a little time."

"Time for what? Did you not feel the yearning, the power of our desire, last night?" He himself had never experienced such with any other woman.

"Everything's been happening so fast. My emotions are on overload—"

Though there was something more, something she wasn't saying....

When yet another camera flash hurt his sensitive eyes, Val was ready to explode. He growled and turned in Irina's direction.

This time, the little redhead approached defiantly, hiding the camera behind her but standing her ground. "There's someone looking for you, Mr. Valentin Kadar. A police detective. I told him to wait in the bar."

"Police?" Adriana echoed faintly.

Irina's expression softened as she regarded her friend. "I'm afraid he wants to talk to you, too, Adriana." Her eyes slid in Val's direction. "Probably about the company you keep."

The police? Val knew he could slip away if he wanted to, could easily drift into the darkness outside. But he couldn't leave Adriana in such a questionable situation.

Even if she was acting as though she hoped he'd disappear.

Adriana felt shaky as she and Val faced Carmine Panchella for the second time. She was certain she already knew what the detective wanted to talk about. In the face of that, all concerns over Stone's sudden appearance blew away with the cool draft of air that seemed to be wafting through the dance club.

"Is there someplace around here where we can have a few words?" Panchella asked, directing the question to Adriana. "Got a key to a private room?"

"I suppose we can use Frank's office," she said. "The manager. Let me ask him."

Frank was amenable to the idea, if curious. But Adriana told him it was a very personal matter. Taking the key, she led Panchella and Val up a flight of stairs and down a dim corridor to the suite on the building's mostly unused second floor.

Frank liked black leather and metal Euro-style furniture combined with extremely modern art.

Panchella took a seat in a chair that resembled an industrial insect about to take flight. Turning up a spindly halogen lamp a couple of notches, Adriana sat behind Frank's shiny black desk while Val eased himself down onto a leather lounger.

Panchella inspected the paintings on the walls—savage splashes of neon colors. "Well, at least there should be enough light in here, even without the lamp." He took out the same ratty notebook he'd used before.

"But let's get down to it. There's been another murder...and another anonymous phone call." He glanced at Val, not attempting to make extended eye contact. "Where were you last night, Mr. Kadar?"

Val frowned. "Another murder?" He seemed genuinely surprised before saying, "I attended the funeral service for Eddie Szewicki last evening. Then I went home."

Adriana nearly started. Why wasn't he mentioning the photo shoot? Walking around Uptown with her? And what about the time they'd spent with Lilly?

She decided to ask the question she most dreaded. "Who was killed, Detective?"

"A young hooker. Blonde, a runaway from some little burg in Wisconsin."

A young blonde from Wisconsin. Adriana tried to swallow the lump in her throat. *Lilly.*

"You know anything about it? Her body turned up near the bus station downtown."

Adriana gazed at Val, who stared back at her, hard, as he spoke up. "Adriana was with me last night."

Panchella scribbled in the notebook. "Ms. Thorn was with you? All night? At your house?"

"That's right."

Panchella raised his brows.

But Adriana was only concerned that Val had withheld information. His mesmerizing glare meant he wanted her to go along. Why? Was he really a murderer, just as she'd feared?

Panchella heaved a sigh. "So you were at the house in Uptown, huh? This phone caller sure has some kinda imagination, let me tell you. He swore he saw the two of you eating at some dive with this girl."

Again, Adriana nearly started. They'd been spied upon. Anxiety over that warred with her initial discomfort at Val's lie. She deliberately refused to look at him. If she wanted to speak, he wasn't going to stop her. But before she could open her mouth, he once again took the lead.

"I believe it is the anonymous troublemaker you should be searching for, Detective," Val said. "He is the one who claims to know all."

"And wants to blame you," said Panchella. "Why?"

Val shrugged. "Perhaps he thinks I'm a good target. I admit I am a loner, that I keep to myself most of the time."

"Except for your lady friend here."

"Except for Adriana," Val agreed, but went on, "Perhaps in the murderer's fevered imagination, I am some kind of night fiend. I assume he mentioned vampires again."

"The girl's body was drained of blood."

"Like Eddie Szewicki's." Val seemed calm, centered, as well as deadly serious. "If you investigate the marks on this newest victim's neck, I am also sure you'll find they were made with the same type of equipment that was used on the unfortunate Eddie. A sick, twisted man is obviously wandering the streets. You must stop him before he strikes down another innocent person."

Was he right? Was there a killer stalking the streets who wanted to implicate Val? Someone who was lurking about, who'd watched them converse with both Eddie and Lilly?

Panchella affixed Val with a hard eye. "Like I said before, you seem to know an awful lot about this case. Maybe you're even acquainted with the guy who's been making these calls."

"There are many people who may have observed me, who may have come to know my habits. The neighborhood in which I live is none too savory."

A nebulous answer, one which didn't satisfy Panchella, if the detective's suspicious expression was any indication.

The reply didn't soothe Adriana, either. Furthermore, she suddenly realized that one or both of the anonymous phone calls might never have happened. Panchella could have made them up as a ploy to get Val to confess. She and Val might be under police surveillance.

Mulling things over, she didn't hear the detective's question until he'd repeated it a second time, "I said, do you have anything to add to this, Ms. Thorn?"

"Hmm?"

"You look upset."

She glanced at Val, who was no longer staring so hard at her. She could lose herself in the gold of those eyes, had tenderly traced the line of those elegant cheekbones with her fingertips, had kissed that wonderful mouth....

She admitted quickly, "Certainly I'm upset. Who wouldn't be at the mention of murder?" But she simply couldn't turn against Val, at least not yet. Perhaps he had a reason for leaving out big chunks of the truth. If nothing else, she wanted to confront him herself first. "I'm also afraid." Either of Val or the person he claimed might be watching everything they did.

Panchella nodded. "I can understand your misgivings. Don't know as I can give you much advice on what to do, though—stick with Kadar or stay away. The anonymous caller seems to be afraid of him, mentioned something about him being the devil incarnate.''

The detective gave Val one last pointed look, but if he was expecting any sort of reaction, he didn't get it.

Instead, Val asked, ''Isn't there a way to trace these phone calls, Detective?''

''Yeah, we're on automatic, getting the numbers—but they've been coming from pay phones.''

''In what neighborhood?''

Panchella smiled tightly. ''I'm asking the questions here, pal.'' He slipped the notebook back into his jacket pocket before standing. ''And since I'm getting next to nowhere, that's about it for now.'' He started to leave, then turned. ''But something ain't right. My gut is giving me weird signals. Like I said before, don't either of you be leaving town.''

''Certainly. We shall be most happy to cooperate.'' Val stood, as well, as if he would politely see the detective out of the building.

Panchella objected, ''I can find my own way,'' and slipped out into the corridor.

Before Val could make another move, Adriana darted out from behind the desk and shut the door. She turned, staring at him accusingly, keeping her voice low. ''You lied!''

''I merely kept some of the truth to myself.''

''What's the difference? We *were* in a restaurant with Lilly last night. And now she's dead!''

His nostrils flared; his eyes seemed to glow. ''And you believe me responsible for the crime? Is that what you're trying to say?''

He looked so fierce, so angry, but Adriana refused to cower, even as she felt a thrill of familiar fear creeping up her spine. ''Lying doesn't help your case any.''

"I was not worried about my case. What I said was meant to protect you."

"Protect me? What are you talking about?"

"You were with me last night, Adriana. Even if there had been no phone call, we would have both been taken down to the police station if I had admitted we had anything to do with that girl. It's likely we may have been put in jail . . . and while I myself can say that I will never spend a day behind bars, I cannot promise the same for you."

"I don't understand."

He waved his hand imperiously, as if he were royalty dismissing a peasant. "You don't have to understand. Things are as they must be. I did what I thought was best for you, and I always will."

Anger burned in her own breast. "Thanks so much, your lordship, but I don't exactly appreciate your high-handed thoughtfulness."

"I am not surprised. You were cold, unhappy with me, before I appeared this evening." He stepped closer, looming over her. "You even feared I would harm your former lover. Have you decided to take him back?"

She willed herself not to flinch before his fiery gaze, but she was caught like a nocturnal animal transfixed by bright light. Blood thrummed in her veins.

Yet she managed to croak, "I already told you I have no interest in Stone!"

He moved even closer, leaning over her until she felt his breath on her face. Her heart thundered in her ears.

"He can never make you feel the way I can, Adriana," he said, voice low, harsh, throbbing. "He can never take you to the highest pinnacle of ecstasy."

Indeed. Her flesh grew warm. Her breasts swelled. Her knees seemed about to give way. She yearned to throw her clothes off right here and now, give herself over to him, a naked, quivering offering.

He raised her chin with one hand, stroked it with a finger, let his lips hover over hers. Longing for his kiss, she opened her mouth, arched her neck, let her eyes drift closed.

Then, just as suddenly, he let her go. "No!"

She nearly collapsed, panted softly, finally opened her eyes.

He stood a few feet away, his back turned toward her. "I want you of your own free will."

Now she was frustrated as well as angry. She straightened, finding her voice. "Meaning you think you can control me?" Over which she felt some doubt herself. To try to assert her own power, put him in his place, she said, "If I was cool when you appeared tonight, it was because I'd already heard about Lilly. It seemed strange that the two of us were the last people to see her alive... just like Eddie."

"So you are back to accusing me of murder. When did I kill this girl? After I took you home?"

She refused to grant him quarter. "I suppose so."

"And why should I kill her?"

"I have no idea. You aren't big on explanations." She supposed he would have to be a psychopath of some sort.

"You *know* that I did not kill Eddie." He spun toward her, the fire in his eyes now mere embers. And he kept some distance between them. "I mourned him with you, paid for his burial."

"True." At least as far as the latter was concerned, anyway.

"I mourn for the little prostitute, as well. Though I cannot make the same gesture for her. It would compromise me . . . and you."

"Right, we don't want to forget that you must protect me," she said, once more moved to sarcasm.

"It is the seemly thing to do, whether or not you dishonor me by accepting another man's attentions."

What an old-fashioned statement. But Adriana was still resentful, dealing with anger. "If you're talking about Stone—again—I'm not even going to bother responding to the accusation."

"Then come home with me, Adriana. Now."

She felt a wave of desire but fought it. "I have another set to do. I'm working."

"I can wait until you're through."

"I don't think so. It'll be better if we put some space between us for a while." Perhaps they should even part forever.

She expected him to be furious, but he remained detached, cool. "All right. I will leave if that is what you truly want."

She swallowed, again seeking strength. "I think it's best."

"Then I bid you farewell."

She moved away from the door and he paused with his hand on the knob, an odd expression in his lustrous gold-brown eyes. She could swear they looked haunted.

"Be careful, Adriana," he warned her. "There *is* a twisted man roaming the streets, someone who hates me. I do not think he would dare harm you, but he is aware of your existence."

Like Panchella, she couldn't help wondering if Val were acquainted with the murderer. "Are you sure you don't know anything about this guy?"

"He is obviously a madman."

An indirect answer because he himself was the real madman? Or was he making a conjecture?

"Take taxis home," he went on. "Don't spend your time alone." He added, "And if you actually encounter danger, think of me. I'll know where you are. I will come."

"What do you mean—you'll know where I am?"

But he was gone, his step so light she heard no noise in the dark corridor outside.

Thoroughly creeped out by just about everything that had gone down that evening, Adriana collapsed in the insect chair and fought against tears. The curious weakness she'd felt the night before seemed to be returning.

Murder. Danger. Darkness both without and within.

For she must be self-destructive. Otherwise, she wouldn't have found the one man on earth who could very well make an ex-boyfriend like Stone look like an amateur. Stone might swindle and pilfer, threaten if he had to, but he avoided anger and violence.

Darkness.

Even with her distrust, her fear, Adriana could only focus on Val's departure, try to fight the overwhelming longing for him to return. The pain inside her was like an open wound.

CHAPTER NINE

His heart heavy, his outlook grim, Val spent two nights roaming the city. On one hand he found himself regretting he'd given Adriana a free choice; on the other, he knew he would never be satisfied with anyone else where a woman was concerned.

Not anymore.

He also told himself that if he really cared about Adriana, he should be willing to let her go. After all, their liaison would probably only lead to unhappiness.

His main concern should be the retrieval of his family's heirloom, the reason he'd come to Chicago in the first place. With time on his hands combined with anger and grief, he searched for his enemy with renewed purpose.

On the second night, around midnight, he located Miklos Rakosi's floating craps game. Having spread some money around the homeless community who wandered the streets near the Chicago River—a larger amount than necessary because Adriana had pricked his conscience on giving alms—Val heard about the gambling taking place in a deserted warehouse.

Two burly men stood guard outside the rundown brick building.

"Who are you?" one asked Val. "You don't get inta this party unless you're on the list."

"I'm not on the list. But I will enter, anyway."

The thug took issue, reaching for the bulge beneath his jacket that must have been a gun. "I don't think so."

Before the weapon could be drawn, Val seized the man, throwing him back against the brick so hard, he whacked his head. As his companion sank unconscious to the concrete, the other guard whipped his gun out but found his trigger hand locked in a grip of iron.

"Ow-w! Damn it, you're breakin' my bones!"

Which was all the scoundrel managed to gasp before Val struck him, sending him lurching to the ground, as well.

Taking one of the guns, a weapon he neither feared nor respected but thought would best serve his purposes for the moment, Val then opened the warehouse door.

Smoke hung low over the motley group of a dozen or so men who either crouched or stood about as one of Rakosi's gang rolled the dice. No one turned a hair until someone noticed that Val was holding a gun on the group. Then there was a sudden silence, a stiffening of posture. Hands moved toward pockets or jackets, where Val knew other weapons resided.

He brandished his own pistol menacingly. "Do not try anything. I will shoot you where you stand. Where is Miklos Rakosi? My business is with him."

Heads turned to the dice roller.

"I don't know where he is," the man stated. "He ain't showed up here yet tonight."

"When is he expected?"

"Don't know that, either."

Val approached Rakosi's henchman, keeping his eyes on the surrounding host, no doubt all unsavory characters. "You had better not be lying."

"I never argue with a gun."

"Bullet holes are not the worst injury you can suffer."

To illustrate his point, Val grasped the dice roller by the throat, lifting him easily, one-handed. Training his eyes and the gun on the audience, he let the man hang, feet dangling, arms swinging at his sides uselessly, mouth gurgling as he choked. Fear paled many faces and the crowd drew back, murmuring.

Which made Val glower even more fiercely and bare his teeth. "I issue a warning—tell Rakosi to return the item he stole from the Kadars and I will leave him alone. If not, he will soon wish he had died and gone to hell."

Lastly, he threw the man directly into the throng, knocking several to the floor. There were yells and curses, a low grunt from the dice roller as he regained his breath. A shot rang out as Val exited, but the bullet merely whizzed past his ear.

Outside, he sought the shadows and tossed his own borrowed weapon into the river. Good riddance. One less danger to a society that possessed far too many of such things.

Meanwhile, he scanned the area to find a hiding place with a good view of the warehouse—the roof of a building seemed suitable. Not that lurking and waiting would do much good. The treasure Rakosi possessed gave him special sensibilities.

Eventually, though, Val knew his path and Rakosi's would cross. When that happened, he would likely have to risk his very existence to regain what had been stolen from him.

Not that life looked so inviting without someone with whom to share it.

Once more, Val felt Adriana's loss like a stab through the heart.

* * *

"In matters of the heart, I see that there is only one woman you will ever love," Irina told a customer who'd paid to hear his fortune according to the tarot.

Passing by the booth, Adriana was surprised when Irina glanced up to catch her eye, making a subtle but urgent gesture that meant she wanted to talk when the reading was finished.

Adriana nodded and pointed to the bar, indicating she'd wait there. Taking a seat on one of the tall stools, she ordered her usual tonic water from Peter, who was full of gossip about mutual acquaintances.

After a minute or two, he brought up the subject he really wanted to discuss. "Heard you and Stone Drake used to live together. That true?"

"Uh-huh," Adriana admitted reluctantly, not having taken any action on the Stone matter yet. And Irina had been the only club employee with whom she'd ever said much about Stone, even when she and the performance artist had been sharing an apartment. "I'd really rather not talk about Stone Drake, if you don't mind."

"I see." Peter winked. "Must be kinda tricky with the new guy hanging around and all."

Adriana made no response to that, relieved when Peter was called away to make some fancy frozen daiquiris.

She already knew the whole staff of After Dark was buzzing about her and "her two men." They were especially curious about the tall, dark Hungarian and why she and Val had been questioned by a detective the night before. To Frank, she'd hinted that it had been part of the continuing investigation surrounding Eddie Szewicki.

It had been the strange situation with the murders that had made her decide to wait on talking to Frank about Stone. Since Val had threatened her ex-boyfriend and seemed to be a serious suspect with the police, she thought it best to avoid making waves.

Naturally, she also intended to avoid Stone himself. Which seemed surprisingly easy. For some reason—the threats from Val?—Stone was concentrating on his job and leaving her alone.

Val. She wondered where he was, what he was doing. After their argument and his cool departure, she seemed to be operating in a restless, drifting fog.

Not that she'd forgotten about the violence that seemed to lurk beneath his surface.

Or his claim that he had an enemy who was dangerous. Playing it safe, she'd taken a taxi home the night before and intended to do the same this evening. She also tried to be aware of the people who surrounded her.

Now she glanced about at the crowd, noticing nothing different or out of the ordinary... unless it was Irina scurrying toward her with an intense expression on her face.

"Come on." Irina grabbed hold of her arm. "I've got something to show you."

"Where are we going?"

"The ladies' lounge. I need some light, and Meggie will let us use her table."

Meggie was the young woman who had a jewelry business set up in the bathroom's anteroom. When customers checked their makeup and hair, she was ready to sell accessories to go with their outfits.

Adriana drew up one of the few chairs in the lounge, while Meggie offered Irina another.

Irina had barely hit the seat before she was pulling out a packet of photographs. She laid five on the jewelry table, looked around and lowered her voice. "I had these developed at one of those overnight places."

"Uh-huh." Adriana stared at the snapshots, all of which seemed to be of her in a purple scarf and dress poised against a backdrop of club crowd. A couple of the photos also included Stone, one with his face turned away from the camera. "So?"

"I took these last night." Irina pointed. "*He* isn't in any of them."

"Are you talking about Val?" Adriana faintly remembered the sudden flashes from the camera now.

"Of course I'm talking about Val." Irina looked disgusted. "He was there, but he's not in the pictures, is he? And I can guarantee you he wouldn't appear in any mirror, either."

Adriana frowned at such wild theory. "What are you trying to say? First, he has no aura and now—"

"He's probably not even alive."

Not alive? Too much. Adriana shook her head. "Come on. I admit these were probably taken last night." When she'd worn the purple outfit. "But you must have clicked the button when Val stepped away or something. I've never heard of a person who couldn't be photographed."

"Well, you're hearing of one now." Irina lowered her voice yet another notch. "I think he's *undead,* Adriana."

Undead? "Come on," she muttered again, wondering if Irina had flipped. "Val takes photographs himself. He's an unusual person, I admit, but—"

"Look at this!" the Gypsy interrupted with a hiss, stabbing one of the photos with her fingernail. "Look closer—you're talking to someone but there's no one there."

Adriana leaned closer, squinting. She conceded she did seem to be talking in the snapshot at issue, but Val must have been out of range. For no particular reason, she also noticed a big, scruffy-looking guy staring at her from the background.

"I've been talking to my Aunt Ludmilla," Irina was going on breathlessly. "She's found out who the Kadars are. They come from an isolated corner of northeastern Hungary, from the foothills of the Carpathians. And they have a long and violent history."

Adriana thought about her conversation with Val the night of Eddie's service. "Most Eastern European countries have a long and violent history. There were always invasions."

"Though none touched the realm of the Kadars. Not the Mongols or the Turks. Not anybody. Want to know why?"

"I expect you intend to tell me."

Irina's eyes flashed with temper, but she seemed intent on controlling it. "You're not taking this seriously. And you should! You're in mortal danger." She leaned closer to stare at Adriana. "Look at you. Your skin is chalk white and there's circles under your eyes."

"I'm wearing black... and not much makeup." Not to mention that she was frazzled, not having slept well.

"Your condition comes from more than a lack of makeup—what have you been doing with him?"

Adriana's heart fluttered a little, recalling the night of passion she and Val had spent together. She *had* been tired and dizzy the next morning. But Val was supposed to be... undead? She couldn't utter the word.

She cleared her throat. "Are you inferring that Val's a vampire?" First the anonymous caller, now her own friend. Even in her weird state of mind, Adriana was beginning to feel angry. "That's a ridiculous premise. I've always been lukewarm about the supernatural. And I'm certainly not willing to invest myself in something so outrageous as believing there are undead people who drink blood." She managed a halfhearted laugh and attempted sarcastic humor. "Good grief, Val doesn't even wear a cape. And he doesn't sleep in a dirt-lined coffin, either. I've been to his house."

If she expected Irina to argue, she was surprised.

Instead, the redhead heaved a big sigh. "Just listen, will you? Let me tell you about the Kadars." Adriana giving her the nod, she continued. "In the thirteenth century, when the Mongols rode into Hungary from Asia, they laid waste to everything before them. There was a Magyar nobleman—a prince, a duke...I don't know what they called them then—who was willing to do anything to save his realm. Supposedly, he made a pact with the devil himself."

"And the nobleman was a Kadar?"

"*The* Kadar. Eventually, the pact included his whole family. When enemies approached, camping out on the plains below Kadar's castle and the walled town—a little place called Kisvarka—they were attacked in the black of night by beings they believed to be demons...a dark horde with glowing eyes mounted on horses whose nostrils steamed with the smoke of hell. In the morning, bodies littered the camp grounds. Not one drop of blood was left in them, not one bone remained unbroken. Most of them were headless. Needless to say, the next wave of warriors retreated, strewing salt behind them."

Adriana couldn't help remarking dryly, "Good tale."

"The same story was repeated by the Turks in the sixteenth century," Irina insisted, "and by several units of Nazis in World War II—though German commanders gave more logical excuses, something about tainted water killing a bunch of soldiers and the town not offering any real threat. Regardless of the reasons, the Kadars' land was never overrun. Kisvarka is the only Hungarian town that was never damaged by sword or gunfire. It has the country's only intact medieval church."

Mongols. Turks. Nazis. Adriana wasn't sure how to react. Again, she thought about Val's discussion of invasions, his mentioning something about the strong measures his domain had had to take. But her modern mind simply couldn't accept such wild and crazy ideas.

Finally, she said lamely, "A nice church, huh? That's an odd outcome for a pact with the devil."

"The thirteenth century priests of Kisvarka were excommunicated for accepting Kadar's unholy pact, for looking the other way," said Irina. "As well they should have been. Kadar might be considered a hero by his own people, but vampires are horrible monsters, predators, murderers who prey on their own kind."

Murderers. Real monsters. Adriana knew they existed but she couldn't believe that any of them were vampires.

Irina believed in vampires, however, and the redhead doubtlessly thought she was trying to be of help. Not wanting to hurt her friend, wishing she could sidestep the ludicrous issue, Adriana stared at the photos again, noticing that the big scruffy man appeared in a second snapshot, too. Dressed in a cheap polyester suit, he seemed out of place in the club scene and his heavy brows were drawn into a mean-looking expression.

"Did I hear someone mention vampires?" Meggie waltzed over, having finished showing bangle bracelets to some customers. She giggled, obviously thinking the other two women had been joking. "I don't have any garlic necklaces, but I have some earrings made of real roses." She opened a small box, revealing unusual post earrings formed of layers of deep red petals. "Vampires aren't supposed to like this kind of flower, you know."

"They aren't?" Adriana knit her brows. Hadn't Val said he was allergic to roses . . . ?

Irina interrogated Meggie, "How did you hear about the power of the rose?"

"There's a lot of vampire books out now," said the jewelry seller. "Even romances with vampire heroes. I read a lot." But she obviously wanted to sell her wares. She picked up one of the red earrings. "See? The petals have been coated with liquid resin and glued to a papier mâché base. Aren't they cool?"

Adriana took the earring, admiring the design.

Irina merely frowned. "It's more likely to be the odor of the rose that bothers vampires. The flower should be newly cut, or, even better, alive. In Romania, they used to plant rosebushes on the graves of people they suspected might rise and walk after dark."

Continuing to feel uncomfortable with the conversation, Adriana desperately searched for a way out. "Still, roses might make a good hedge against vampires. They probably don't like the flower in any condition." That statement of faith should surely comfort Irina. She reached into the little purse she always slung about her shoulders at work. "How much are these earrings, Meggie? I feel like wearing them tonight."

After the jewelry seller had made change and flitted off to talk to another customer, Irina put in a last warning word. "Watch out for Kadar, Adriana. He seeks to enthrall you, to make you his own. He's probably lonely after all these centuries." She added, "But he's also hungry. *He's* the one who killed Eddie and merely paid for the service to impress you."

Now that was enough. "There were no bite marks on Eddie's throat. His blood was drained by some type of equipment, not a vampire."

"Is that what the brute told you?"

"That's what the police say. But the information is confidential—don't tell anyone else." Adriana wasn't about to bring up the second murder or that she questioned Val's innocence herself. Irina rarely listened to the news or read papers, so it should be easy enough to get her off the trail. "I appreciate your advice, but you don't have to worry about me and Val. We broke up last night."

The redhead's eyes widened. "He allowed you to do that?"

Adriana fought irritation, then the intense sadness that swept over her every time she thought about sending Val away. "He doesn't have to grant me the right for anything, Irina. I can do what I want. I'll probably never see Valentin Kadar again."

Until... If she decided to end the estrangement. Or unless she found herself in the type of danger that Val would "sense" and take it upon himself to appear. But then, by claiming he could do such a thing, it only proved he might be crazy, whether or not in a dangerous way.

* * *

Miklos Rakosi feared Stone Drake might be too sly and weak to deal with real danger. Yet the young man needed money and, since he worked with Adriana Thorn and knew her so well, he seemed the best person to keep an eye on Kadar's mistress. Rakosi had approached Drake the evening before, after overhearing the interesting conversation between Drake and Adriana.

He fingered the medallion hanging about his neck with a little smile, once more appreciating the powers it gave him, like a heightened sense of hearing. Not to mention the ability to avoid detection beneath Kadar's very nose.

Unfortunately, the medallion's protection was limited if Rakosi faced Kadar in a one-to-one confrontation. That's why he'd been trying to attack his enemy in indirect ways.

But if the phone calls to the police continued to fail, Rakosi would not hesitate to use Adriana. A little after midnight, the second night in a row, he dropped by After Dark to talk to Drake, a henchman in tow, though Weasel had been getting on his nerves of late, always whining.

They found the bouncer surveying the dance floor.

"Did you follow Adriana Thorn home last night?" Rakosi asked.

Drake eyed the two men, unsmiling. "Yeah, she took a taxi and went right inside." He added, "I had to take a taxi, too. Kind of expensive. Do I get extra compensation for that sort of thing?"

Money, money, money. With far more at stake, Rakosi could not help reacting impatiently to such obvious greed. "You are being paid quite adequately, especially considering you have not really been asked to do anything."

"You said I was supposed to keep an eye on Adriana."

"And do whatever else I ask, as well. If the occasion arises, you may have to seize the woman and bring her to me."

"Seize her?" Drake frowned. "What do you plan to do to her?"

"That is not your problem." Rakosi could see the weakness surfacing in the young man again. Attempting to use another frailty to counteract it, he pulled out his wallet to remove several bills. "Here, take the extra compensation you demand—there will be much more to come. Though you will do as I order when I say so."

Drake grabbed the money but looked none too happy. Again Rakosi felt doubt surface, wondering if he had made a mistake. If so, Drake would be the one to suffer.

At that same moment, a low ringing erupted from Rakosi's jacket pocket and he cursed in Hungarian. He moved off to a corner for privacy so he could answer his small cellular phone. When he could understand the hysterical words flung at him so swiftly, when he realized that Kadar had visited the craps game, he was appalled. He hung up, knowing he had to move the *Buckthorn* immediately. The boat was docked far too near the invaded warehouse, mere blocks away. He didn't want to lose his entire center of operations, his home.

He went outside, looking for his car.

"Hey, boss," said Weasel, nearly running to keep up with Rakosi's longer strides. "If you want something done to that woman, I'm your man. You don't need some bozo like that bouncer. He ain't got any nerve."

"I am not worried about the woman at the moment." He was concerned for his own skin. "There is trouble to deal with."

But Weasel paid no attention, whining on. "I could use some extra money myself."

The dolt was desperate, had lost too much at playing craps himself. But Rakosi wasn't in the mood to deal with anyone else's problems. "I have no time for this."

"Listen, I'll undercut the guy." Weasel's beady eyes glittered in his narrow face. "How much are you paying him? I'll do it for less."

"Shut up!" At the end of his patience, Rakosi finally turned to strike the man, only to have Weasel skitter backward as fast as the stinking, slippery little animal for which he was named. He obviously knew Rakosi's great strength could cripple him with one blow. "Bah! Stay here, then, if you cannot behave."

Furious as well as nervous, Rakosi slid into the car and took off, leaving Weasel to fend for himself.

Adriana got through the rest of the night at After Dark by losing herself in music. She played a haunting mix of rock and melodic jazz, danceable most of the time, except for short parts that faded into the sound of the wind blowing through a dark forest.

She felt as if she were wandering through a forest herself. Alone. She couldn't talk to Irina and she didn't want to talk to Frank. She didn't feel like walking about and striking up conversations with customers.

And she wanted to avoid Stone Drake at all costs. Again, though, her ex-boyfriend kept his distance. He didn't even approach her when she left the place around three-thirty.

Conveniently for once, a taxi waited right outside the club. The driver perked up as soon as he saw her, reaching behind him to open the door invitingly. "Where to?"

Adriana gave him the address and settled back as the vehicle took off. As they headed down Chicago Avenue, which would soon pass the little park and the Water Tower, she thought of the first night she and Val had met, the first time he'd kissed her. No, she corrected herself, that was the time she'd imagined him kissing her....

Intent on her thoughts, she nevertheless noticed when the driver made a swift turn down a side street. "Hey, I said Oak Street. That's north of here, not south."

Beady eyes stared at her in the rearview mirror. "Don't worry, lady. I know where I'm going."

Something was very wrong. Glancing at the ID above the taxi's meter—which wasn't running—Adriana saw that the visage in the photo didn't match this narrow-faced driver's.

Panicking, she grabbed the door handle. "Let me out of here!"

Which caused the driver to brake so hard, she nearly fell to the floor. With a swift, hard backhand, he smacked her in the face. She sank down in the seat, seeing stars.

As she half lay there, he put the car in park and ripped off her dark scarf to tie her wrists. "Now are you gonna come quietly or do I have to stuff your mouth, too?"

She could only murmur something unintelligible.

"That's a good girl." But he was talking mainly to himself. "Soon as the boss sees I've got Kadar's little honey, I'll be back on his good side. And make some money to boot."

He put the taxi into gear again and peeled out.

Kadar's little honey? Boss?

Did the driver work for the mysterious enemy of Val's? The man who'd been making the phone calls, who'd no doubt killed Eddie and Lilly? Would he now kill her? How ironic—after Val had told her she should take taxis for safety's sake.

She only wished Val *could* suddenly appear, because she certainly was in danger....

As the taxi careered around a corner, Adriana managed to hoist herself into an upright position, just in time to see the vehicle head straight for a pedestrian stepping out of the shadows.

She cried out, and the driver yelled as the taxi came to a jarring halt. Adriana was thrown forward, then backward, then sideways. She rolled onto the floor.

Metal crunched and squealed as if being torn.

The driver screamed, "Ya-ah!" And screamed yet again as an animal snarled.

Snarling? What in the world? Heart pounding, more frightened than ever, Adriana dragged herself to a sitting position. The left front door lay on the pavement near the driver. Someone tall was bending over his body.

Adriana blinked, certain she recognized the set of those proud shoulders. "V-Val?"

He came to the car immediately, opened the passenger door and saw her disheveled state. "What has happened? What has this man done to you?"

"He tried to pull off a kidnapping." She held up her wrists, and he tore the scarf away, then helped her out and onto her feet. "Is he dead?"

"Only unconscious."

She leaned against him, shaky. "Wh-what are you doing here, anyway?" Had he actually sensed her danger?

"I was on my way to the club. I knew you would probably not wish to speak to me, but I wanted to be near you, even if it could only be from a distance."

Luckily for her, Val hadn't given up so easily.

He glared at the fallen driver. "This fool nearly ran over me."

"There wasn't a collision?" She hadn't heard a thud. "He didn't hit you?"

"He hit his own head...against the windshield as he came to a screeching stop."

"And the door?"

"Perhaps it had rusted through. It fell off when he staggered outside."

How strange. "But he was screaming—"

"Because he was obviously in pain."

She didn't think she wanted to bring up the snarls. Perhaps, in her woozy state, she'd only imagined them.

Val was glancing around. "We waste time. There is another taxi at the stop sign over there—it has been idling for several minutes. He is probably calling in this accident."

"Meaning the police will be arriving soon."

They walked away, Adriana struggling to keep up with Val's long strides as they darted down a shadowy alley. Maybe they should have stayed so she could tell the police what happened to her. Maybe that would have lessened suspicion against Val. In less than two blocks, they emerged onto Chicago Avenue again and flagged down a real taxi.

"Where to?"

Adriana surprised herself a little by blurting out Val's address. Why not? Leaning against the hard wall of his chest, resting her head on his shoulder, she felt truly safe.

Valentin Kadar wasn't a murderer. The botched kidnapping proved that. He'd been telling the truth about having a terrible enemy.

CHAPTER TEN

Adriana waited until the taxi dropped them off at Val's house to vent her worries. "There is a twisted murderer watching us, isn't there? And he has people working for him. The kidnapper said I was your honey and that he was taking me to his boss—"

Val interrupted, "We must get you inside, take care of your cheek. It is swelling. There will be a bad bruise."

Bruises were hardly on the same level with murder, but Adriana truly was feeling wrung out and appreciated his attentions. Val lifted her easily and carried her up the steps of the porch. The door opened smoothly as he touched the lock.

The house was dark as usual, but Val had no problem finding the antique couch. He laid her carefully against the cushions, switched on the little brass lamp and told her he was going to the kitchen to get some ice.

When he returned, he knelt beside the couch and placed a cold pack against her cheek. "There, that should help it feel better."

She winced.

"I am so sorry that man hurt you." His low voice made her spine tingle. "At least his face will be bruised, as well."

"From hitting his head?" She couldn't help having an inkling there had been more; she hadn't quite been able to forget those snarls. "You didn't do anything to him?"

"Nothing an abductor did not deserve."

"But you weren't aware that I was in the taxi at first, were you? You said the driver staggered out of the vehicle and fell on his own." Not unless Val had actually sensed she was in danger....

He asserted, "I could tell he was up to no good." As if that remark would settle things. Then he stroked her good cheek, creating a warmth that spread as far as her fingers and toes. "Would you like a glass of wine, Adriana? Or some cognac? It will dull the pain."

She could use a drink. "Cognac or brandy would be great."

"Then I shall get it for you."

He rose to glide toward some shelves that stood against one wall of the room, leaving her with a slight sense of unease. Though she appreciated his ministrations and the safety he seemed to offer, she only wished she could trust him completely. There was always this undercurrent of something hidden, secret—even violent—about Val. In her mind's eye, she saw him picking men up and throwing them as if they were rag dolls—the guy who'd tried to take her taxi, then Lilly's pimp a couple of nights ago. Now there was this newest incident, whether or not the kidnapper merited what he'd gotten.

Val poured two glasses of cognac, one of which he placed on the table beside the lamp. The other he offered to Adriana as he knelt beside her again.

Their fingers grazed as she took the glass and she nearly melted from the banked fire in his eyes. She blinked and took a sip as he brushed back her hair with a tender gesture.

"Where did you get these?"

It took her a moment to realize he meant the new earrings she'd purchased and put on earlier. She gazed at him closely, noting his frown. "There's a young woman who sells jewelry at After Dark. Do you like them?"

"Roses aren't my favorite flower."

"I seem to remember you saying something about an allergy."

His pallor was noticeable against the shadows in the room.

"You don't happen to be allergic to the sun, too?" she inquired, thinking about the ridiculous conversation she'd had with Irina. Unfortunately, the tales had been as unforgettable as they'd been wild. "I've never seen you out and about except at night. You said you never meet people for lunch."

He admitted, "I do have a sun allergy."

"Really? How strange."

"Not so strange. Merely the result of a rare blood disease that runs in my family."

Rare blood disease? At that disclosure, Adriana felt a thrill that had nothing to do with Val's touch. But she couldn't bring herself to even think about such things as vampires.

"This disease is another reason I take herbs," Val informed her.

The herbs. She'd never heard of any connected with vampires. But she told herself to think more scientifically and tried to ask an intelligent question. "Does this same disease give you night vision? You seem to need less light than anyone I've ever known."

"I have always had little trouble finding my way about in the dark." He adjusted the ice pack, adding,

"You really should remove the earrings, Adriana. They look fragile. I do not wish to damage them."

"Why don't you remove them?" She hated to be manipulative, but she wanted to see what he would do.

If she expected a startled stare or sizzling flesh, she was absolutely wrong. Val let her hold the ice pack while he carefully removed the posts. Then he stood and stepped over to the fireplace to place the earrings on the mantel.

Perfectly natural behavior. Which made her relax a bit. Unless it was actually the aroma of the living flower that drove the undead crazy....

The undead? Bunk! Vampires were only creatures of fiction.

Concentrating on Val, the man, Adriana took a deep breath as he returned to pick up his glass of cognac and pull a chair close to the couch. He took a sip. She'd seen him eat, if sparingly. Drinking and eating weren't activities associated with vampires. She should tell Irina that the next time her friend made bizarre accusations.

Meantime, she continued to focus on Val as he reached across to reexamine her cheek. His long, sensitive fingers left trails of heat. Her neck throbbed where he had bitten her.

Bitten. Damn. After finally getting comfortable, she felt uneasiness rise again. Probably because she couldn't help thinking of the throat wounds on both murder victims. Val had changed the subject when she'd mentioned the killer earlier. Did he actually know the guy's identity or not?

Stirring, she moved back against the cushions and away from the distraction of his touch. "This killer who's draining people's blood and making it look like a vampire—"

He nodded. "The madman."

She took a couple of swigs of cognac to fortify herself. "Are you certain you don't know anything about him? He seems to have a personal vendetta against you...and anyone you're associated with." She reflected, "Not to mention that he doesn't seem to fit the description of the average serial killer. They don't usually hire other people to work for them."

"That is indeed odd."

"Who would want to do you damage? Surely it's more than some deranged individual who observed your nocturnal habits and decided it might be fun to blame some grisly killings on you."

"I agree. That concerns me and, after what happened tonight, surely must frighten you. But do not worry. I will protect you."

"A sentiment that's very touching," she had to admit. "Though hardly enough." Not when other people had been killed. And when Val wasn't really answering her questions.

He glowered, his brows drawing together. "It is not enough to offer you protection? What do you want, then? The man impaled on a spear?"

She nearly choked on her cognac. "Ugh, how horrible! Why on earth would you think of something like that?"

"You must pardon me, Adriana, but I come from an old-world culture. My family is an ancient one. A Magyar respects the way of the warrior, protects his own whether in war or feud."

His family. Magyar warriors.

Those words brought up a vision of the night-cloaked, glowing-eyed horde Irina had described so vividly. She lowered the ice pack. "War? Feud? You are hinting that the murderer really is carrying out a vendetta, aren't you? Does he have something to do with your family?"

"You are jumping to conclusions. Upsetting yourself."

"I'm upset, sure." Tears sprang to her eyes. "A friend of mine is dead, as well as a mixed-up young girl who could have started a new life."

At that, he seemed to sink back into the chair. He sighed deeply. "I grieve for the horrible things that have happened, too." He sounded absolutely sincere, somber, distressed. "And I cannot forgive myself that a killer has taken people you knew... that he terrorizes you. But again I question what I can do. Except to try to stop similar incidents from happening."

"Then you've decided you're going to work with the police?" For no matter what he said—or avoided saying—she couldn't help but believe he knew more than he was admitting.

"The police." He made a derisive sound. "You regard such authorities as invincible, hmm?" Then he rose and walked out of the room.

"Val!"

Now what? Confused, frustrated, intent on finishing their conversation, Adriana laid the ice pack aside and attempted to follow him. In the gloom of the dining room, she ran smack into the stack of heavy boxes she'd noticed before. One tumbled off, hitting the floor with a big thud, spilling something dark.

She stooped and probed with an exploring finger, surprised when she realized the contents of the box was dirt. Dirt? For lining a coffin?

Now agitated, as well as confused, she entered the kitchen and stared at the crumbs of soil beneath her fingernails. Val was giving the dog a bowl of water. The friendly looking animal saw her and wagged his tail.

"He is much better," Val told her, not remarking on the thud he must have heard from the other room.

She struggled to find her voice, unable to bring up the topic of dirt just as yet. There simply had to be a logical explanation.

She gazed at the dog. "He looks better, has some shine to his coat." Which was midnight black. "Are the cats okay, as well?"

"There seem to be more of them every day. And I have a young owl nesting in the study."

"An owl?"

"It hurt its wing, but it is recovering."

"You've got quite a menagerie."

To whom he showed tolerance and affection in his own way. What a contrast to all the talk of murder and vendettas...and the ridiculous thoughts about vampires.

"I have always appreciated animals, even in Hungary," Val went on. "They are elemental, in some ways far wiser than humans."

Despite herself, Adriana was reminded of Irina's warnings. "What part of Hungary are you from, anyway?"

"A remote area in the northeast." He opened a creaky-hinged cabinet to take out some storage containers and a large unopened bag of cat food. "You will not have heard of it."

Maybe, maybe not. "Is it anywhere near the town of Kisvàrka, the place that has the intact medieval church?"

"Have you been reading about Eastern Europe?"

"Someone told me about Kisvarka this very night. They also repeated a legend about the Kadars, a family that lives there—"

"There are many Kadars in Hungary."

"Kadars that drove away Mongols and Turks and Nazis? Kadars that people fear?"

He didn't answer as, expression unreadable, he opened the bag of cat food and reached into yet another cabinet to collect more bowls.

Then he moved toward the back door. "Excuse me. I will return in a moment."

What a strange man.

A strange house.

A strange situation.

She gazed around the dilapidated kitchen with its aged cabinetry and appliances. Idly, she examined the glass containers on the counter, noting one seemed to hold paprika, another some type of seeds, while a third seemed full of crushed green and brown stuff.

The herb mixture Val used for his blood disease?

On a whim, she opened the container and removed a big pinch. She tasted it, wrinkling her nose at the bitter taste, then sprinkled the rest into a tissue she had in the pocket of her lightweight coat. For what reason, she wasn't certain...but when she heard the doorknob turning, she hastily replaced the top on the container so Val wouldn't know what she had done.

She moved away to pat the dog as he wagged his tail harder. "You're a sweetheart, aren't you, baby?" She straightened, announcing to Val, "Now back to this murderer. What did you mean by saying you wanted to stop him but that the police aren't invincible? Are you or are you not going to try to work with them? You can't fight the killer yourself."

"I do not like dealing with authorities."

"Oh, great, then you're thinking of proceeding on your own." She confessed, "That scares me, Val." Speaking of fear. "*You* scare me." For more reasons than she was willing to say. "You don't seem to turn a hair at the mention of violence."

"Some violence is natural. There has always been prey and predator in nature."

"But you're not a predator." Was he? "There has to be another solution than violence."

"You are worried about wrongdoers? They are the only people I intentionally threaten."

Meaning he unintentionally threatened other people?

He went on, "If you'd gotten the chance, would you not have struck back at your abductor tonight, Adriana?"

"I—I'm not sure." But wouldn't she have hit him with a big purse if she'd had one? Kicked and punched at him if she'd seen a chance to get away?

Even as she pondered that, Val explained, "Fighting back in some situations is natural. I am a man of the old world, someone who battles for his own—my land, my family...my woman."

His woman.

"I am referring to you, Adriana," he said, even as she dwelled upon his exciting words.

For though she was a modern woman, such an old-fashioned statement of possession appealed to her at a deep, primeval level. Her pulse threaded unevenly.

He went on, "I could not contain my temper when I overheard Stone Drake express his devotion to you."

Stone? But she should be glad he'd brought up her ex-boyfriend. Now that was one situation where threats wouldn't do.

She told him, "You didn't hear me confess anything back, did you? Besides, Stone wasn't being serious. He's full of it."

Val frowned. "Full of what?"

"I'm using an idiom." Obviously one he didn't recognize. "It means he's full of, um, waste materials."

He raised his brows. "I only know that you tried to protect him and turned against me. That hurt me, Adriana."

"I didn't turn against you," she objected. "I just wanted to avoid trouble. Stone is a thief but he's not a fighter. And you're—" She hesitated, trying to figure out how to put it. "You're very, very strong. I saw you pick up a man more than once and throw him several yards away."

"I was angry. When adrenaline surges, one never knows what might happen."

Could simple adrenaline really do that? she wondered for a moment, then forgot about everything but Val as he stepped closer.

He took her chin in his hand. "You have a beautiful heart and soul, Adriana. You are too good for the likes of Stone." He added, golden eyes bright but haunted, "You are much too good for the likes of me."

How could she not respond? Her pulse thrummed as he leaned over her. "I—I'm not perfect." Furthermore, "But you have to have good inside yourself or you couldn't recognize it in someone else."

Again, her heart told her Val couldn't be a bad man. A little dangerous, maybe…when that adrenaline of his surged. And most definitely mysterious.

He ran a finger over her lips, then kissed them, letting out a long, slow breath. "So sweet, like nectar from a flower."

Desire stirred, trembled, rose from deep within. Her surroundings became hazy, her experiences that night melted away, the conversation they'd been having dissolved into the intoxication Val always produced in her.

"Kiss me again," she whispered.

He complied most willingly, taking her in his arms, winding his fingers through her long, thick hair. She let her head loll as he laved her throat with his tongue, moved higher to nip softly at her lips, then covered them with his own. When he deepened the kiss, exploring with his tongue, she wound her arms about his neck and rubbed herself against him.

"Ah, Adriana." He unbuttoned her coat and gazed raptly at the soft flesh mounding above her black bustier. "You are delectable, tantalizing."

She was also warm, wet, aroused. She could feel that he was ready, pressing hard against his trousers. "I want to make love."

"And so we shall. But somewhere more comfortable than this kitchen."

Turning her about, he pressed her tightly against him, back to front, and walked her out into the other room. One of her shoes slipped on the dirt she'd accidentally spilled.

"Sorry, I knocked a box onto the floor," she murmured in the heat of passion.

"It is not important—only materials for landscaping."

Landscaping? So there *had* been a logical explanation.

Reassurance only added flames to the fire that had been started. She moaned as he lowered her to the couch and quickly unlaced the bustier. She arched her back as he suckled at first one breast, then the other. His hands wandered, exploring every inch of flesh, caressing every curve. One by one, he removed each piece of clothing until she lay naked.

She had managed only to unbutton his shirt. Adriana smoothed her hands over the hard planes of his chest, lightly dusted with hair.

Her legs sprawled about his waist, Val leaned forward to take her mouth yet again. But she wanted more, faster. Being intimate with Val drove her to the edge.

She undid his zipper, encircled his heat with her hand, guided him to her.

He growled, joining them with one savage thrust, rocking them in a union that sent her too quickly over the edge.

He was laughing softly when she regained her senses. And still rigid inside her. "Such passion. Though you have a loving heart, you also possess enough selfishness to allow yourself pleasure."

"I'm selfish?"

She wasn't sure she liked that. And she wanted to see him lose himself as completely as she had. Arching her back again, touching him intimately, undulating her hips, she was gratified when those golden eyes grew smoky and unfocused, pleased when he stopped speaking.

He pushed her back against the cushions, thrust faster and faster until she writhed beneath him.

"You are mine!" he cried, looming over her as she rose toward the heights yet a second time.

"More!" she begged, wanting that same sharp rapture she'd felt the first time they'd made love.

He'd already found the sweet spot on her throat. Again the tiny pricks of pain. Again the rush of blood, the sense of floating as she shuddered over and over in release.

She didn't hear the sound of his own satisfaction, must have lost consciousness completely, since when she opened her eyes again, they were upstairs in his bed. Now naked as well, Val cradled her against him.

"Are you all right?" he asked, smoothing her hair with great tenderness. "You tempt me into losing control. It has been so long. It could be too much, too soon."

It had been a long time? She felt deeply complimented, considering what a passionate man he was.

"I wanted to give you as much pleasure as you give me."

"Believe me, Adriana, you grant me pure ecstasy. Our hearts beat as one. Our souls fly." He added, "I will always come when you call me."

He would come when she called.

"Val!" Standing on a windswept beach, Adriana gazed up into the sparkling expanse of a beautiful night sky. "Valentin Kadar!"

Then he was suddenly there, alighting beside her, arms drawing her against him. "My lovely Adriana."

She smiled, gazing into his golden eyes. She was happy, ecstatic, felt as if she were floating off the ground.

Floating.

With only a little surprise, she realized they were floating, rising on an updraft.

"We're flying!"

"Of course. I thought to take you home the scenic way."

And they climbed higher and higher into the glow of moonlight and stars.

"Is this not beautiful?" he asked.

She clung to him. "It's wonderful!"

"I shall show you more."

His jacket fluttering like wings, he extended an arm and turned in the air. They glided forward, speeding above Lake Michigan. Far below, the water glistened, silver and charcoal and dove gray. Waves kissed the shore.

The diamond-studded skyline of the city approached, and Adriana spotted her building facing the outer drive and the beach beyond. "I don't want to go home, not yet."

"Then I shall give you a tour."

They flew on, skimming the tops of tall buildings. The streets spread out, an intricate net of lights. Cars glided down them and tiny figures scurried about, small enough to be dolls.

Val extended his arm again, diving like a hawk. They sped between the highest buildings, viewing crazy angles of glass and steel.

"Oh!" Her hair streaming behind her, she closed her eyes for a moment, dizzy....

Adriana still felt dizzy when she struggled into the club for work on Friday night. She hadn't talked to Val about her incredibly realistic dream of flying, hadn't so much as seen him since she'd fallen asleep in his arms after making love.

This time, she hadn't remembered one detail about returning to her home, though she'd awakened in her own bed the next day at sunset with a bruised face, her hair tangled as if by wind...and blood spotting her pillow.

In the bar, Adriana eased herself down onto a stool and slid a finger beneath her hair to touch the bandage covering the sore, scabby area on her neck. It throbbed and the room spun, making her nauseous. She placed her elbows on the bar, steadying her head in her hands.

"Hey, what's the matter, Adriana?" said Peter. "You look terrible."

It couldn't be the bruise—she'd covered it with thick stage makeup. "I'm okay."

Peter wasn't convinced. "You're real pale. Seen a doctor?" he asked as he moved down the bar to deliver a drink.

"She needs a priest or a minister, not a doctor," murmured a low, familiar voice at Adriana's elbow.

"Irina." She raised her head, the action making her break into a cold sweat. She reached into the pocket of the light coat she'd thrown on tonight, removing a wadded tissue to dab her forehead. "A priest or a minister? Will you stop it already?"

"I'll stop it when you stop seeing Val." Irina gazed at the sprinkles of herb mixture scattered across the polished surface of the bar. Adriana had forgotten she'd crumpled the stuff into the tissue the night before. The redhead asked, "What is that?"

"Uh, nothing."

Irina scooped the herbs into an empty ashtray. "Don't give me the 'nothing' business. This has something to do with Valentin Kadar, doesn't it?"

"They're only herbs that he takes for his digestion."

Which was all the private conversation the women could share before Frank Nieman swept down on them.

"My God, Adriana, Peter is right—you look like a ghost." He actually appeared frightened as he felt her forehead. "You're so cold. You obviously have the chills. Go home, darling. You're very sick."

"But Friday is one of our busiest nights—"

Frank's gaze remained sympathetic behind his wire-framed glasses. "Don't worry, we'll get along. I booked a good band this week and the radio program can simply be canceled for once."

"You're suggesting I take tomorrow night off, too?"

"Unless your health changes drastically." He urged, "Go see a doctor. Put yourself to bed. You may have walking pneumonia or mono and not be aware of it."

"I don't think it's that serious." Feeling oddly about the wound on her throat, Adriana didn't want to see a doctor. Though she had to admit slipping into bed sounded awfully good. "I can call you tomorrow."

"If you wish, though I'll be more than understanding if you need time off. I won't so much as dock your pay—you've never missed a shift since you started working here." Frank leaned toward her as if to kiss her on the cheek, then stiffened. "Oops, perhaps I shouldn't do that, just in case whatever you have is catching."

"Frank shouldn't be concerned—I don't think he would appeal to Mr. Kadar," Irina muttered under her breath.

Only Adriana scowled at her friend.

But that didn't stop Irina from accompanying her to the door. "I really wish you'd get off this vampire business."

The redhead paid no attention, looking anxious. "Do you want me to come and stay with you? I could take a good crack at keeping that devil away."

"No." Adriana fought irritation. "I'll be okay." Then she lied, "Besides, I told you we broke up."

"Sure." Irina didn't sound as if she believed that at all. "And even if you weren't going out, he could come to you while you slept."

"Not likely. We have a doorman."

"You think a doorman can stop a vampire?"

"That's enough!" Despite her desire to avoid friction, Adriana couldn't help feeling angry. She turned before heading out to the street to flag down a taxi. "I'm safe, okay? I don't want to hear any more of this heebie-jeebie vampire stuff. Get off it!"

Unused to such a display of aggression from Adriana, Irina shrank back. Adriana ran, head pounding, breath coming short, only pausing to check the ID of the taxi she flagged down to make sure that the driver was who he was supposed to be.

As the vehicle pulled away, she saw Stone run out of the club and hurry directly for her, a strange expression on his face.

"Get lost!" she muttered, giving him a scornful wave.

At least she wouldn't have to listen to any nonsense from her ex-boyfriend tonight. She had much more interesting things to think about.

CHAPTER ELEVEN

Val couldn't stop thinking about Adriana. Their connection was stronger than ever. He was obsessed with her, could barely go about his usual activities without imagining what she was doing at that moment, how she looked, how she felt.

She is the one.

This truth echoed over and over through his mind.

But the truth was dangerous and could mean pain for them both.

Adriana was a good person. Sullying such a lovely creature was a crime against nature. That's why he'd offered her a choice at every step of their relationship.

Yet if she rejected him in the end, condemned him to exist alone in eternal darkness, heartbreak could hardly describe what he would feel upon parting.

Sometimes he wished his existence was simpler. He wished he were still the sort of man who went after what he wanted and took it ruthlessly. But time and wisdom had softened him. Then again, if he were the same man he was years ago, he might not have been able to appreciate Adriana at all. She was too complex, refined and subtle for someone who had not developed keener sensibilities.

But enough. He had his duty to perform, Val reminded himself. For his family's sake, he needed to concentrate on catching Rakosi.

Strolling down a winding street that lay above the Chicago River, Val passed a woman using a pay phone. He stopped near a railing that kept pedestrians from falling into the green-brown water. Below and some yards down was the brick warehouse where the craps game had been held the night before.

The cavernous space was empty now. Rakosi's boat had been moved, as well.

If only Val hadn't been called away, if he'd been able to maintain careful vigilance, he knew he might actually have found the chance to confront his enemy.

But he could never allow danger to threaten Adriana. Enraged that someone would even try, he'd had to call on all his self-control to keep from ripping the head off the lowlife who had dared try to abduct her.

She was his. He could not help feeling so to his very depths. A rich and intoxicating blend of sweetness and spice, Adriana Thorn set his heart aflame.

Which brought up memories of making love—her dark hair fanning about her beautiful face as she'd arched beneath him, the intense cries of pleasure she'd made, her smooth skin....

And, whether he liked it or not, once again Val became immersed in obsessive thoughts of Adriana. He knew she was safe. He would have sensed otherwise. But he wanted to be closer, to touch her sweet flesh and reassure himself anyway.

Closing his eyes, he let his consciousness drift...and *felt* Adriana tossing restlessly, her limbs languorous.

She wasn't at the club, he realized. She was at home in bed, her heart and body filled with intense longing for him.

Longing... damnation!

No more searching for Rakosi tonight. Val couldn't resist the siren call.

But he would at least try to keep the lovely, vulnerable Adriana at a distance, he thought as he headed back for the pay phone.

Adriana had gone home and to bed, but she hadn't been able to sleep. Exhausted, yet strangely alert, she lay against the cool sheets, daydreaming about Val and listening to Phantom purr as the night passed by. The condo was quiet, Jennifer out for a Friday dinner and an overnight with Todd.

Thank goodness her sister had left early, hadn't been around to see her stumbling out of bed. Adriana knew Jennifer would have insisted on taking her to a hospital.

But Adriana didn't believe she was really sick. A little tired she could admit to, along with flustered, dazed and disturbed. But then, who wouldn't be reeling after falling head over heels for a mysterious man like Val...not to mention finding oneself embroiled in a macabre murder mystery.

When the phone rang, she nearly jumped out of her skin. And the cat squalled, leaping off the bed.

Who on earth? Irina? Stone? Not wanting to talk to either friend or antagonist, Adriana let her answering machine pick up. She turned the volume higher to monitor the message.

"Adriana?" The voice was low, throbbing.

With a thrill, a catch of breath, she pounced on the receiver. "Val. You're actually calling me, and you without a phone—"

"You were thinking about me. I felt compelled to answer. Why are you home?"

And how did he know she was? "Frank thought I was too sick to work."

"Are you ill?" he asked, concern edging his voice.

"I was a little dizzy when I woke up, but I'm better now."

"You probably need something to eat. Meat would improve your energy."

"I told you I was a vegetarian."

"Vegetables do not provide the same sustenance. I will meet you at your apartment building and take you to eat."

"When?"

"Five minutes."

"I have to get dressed. Fifteen would be better."

"I shall be waiting outside."

She flung aside the covers and sprang to her feet, surprised she actually didn't feel dizzy anymore. As she quickly pulled on boots, jeans and a red silk blouse, she wondered why Val hadn't asked to come up to her door. He'd delivered her there before.

But then, perhaps he thought Jennifer would be hanging around. He wasn't exactly a gregarious person.

As she came out onto the sidewalk to greet him a few minutes later, the intensity of his eyes deepened. Blood rushing, heart pounding, she looked him over with equal enthusiasm. He was stylish as usual in a dark Armani suit with a silky pale scarf about his neck. The light kiss they shared as a greeting was hardly enough.

"What kind of cuisine would you like?" he asked, taking hold of her shoulders. "Is there a restaurant you prefer near here?"

"I don't want anything fancy." She was hard put to care about food at all with him touching her as he was.

"A sandwich and some soup will do." Just being with Val seemed to feed something deep inside her.

He offered his arm. "Lead the way."

Though she'd rather hold hands, she took his arm, pleased by Val's old-fashioned, old-world charm. Happy to share his company, she ambled toward Michigan Avenue in the direction of a casual restaurant she liked.

A little more than an hour later, around ten o'clock, they'd finished their meal and were back on the streets. Val had insisted she eat meat and, to her surprise, Adriana had managed to down a medium-rare hamburger.

"I can't believe it," she remarked. "That beef actually tasted good, and I'm not feeling sick. People say that red meat sits in your stomach like a lump when you're not used to it."

"You needed something with blood."

She wrinkled her nose. "I hate to think of it that way."

Nevertheless, she was experiencing a burst of energy. But she also attributed the extra vigor to being with Val. He made her pulse rush.

"So where to now?"

Val suggested, "The Night Gallery is open until 2:00 a.m. Some of my photographs are being shown there."

"Why didn't you say so?"

"I had other things on my mind."

The way he was looking at her made her think she had been on his mind. She thought about asking him to return to the condo with her, but decided she wanted to see the photographs first.

The gallery was located only a little west and north of After Dark, so the distance was quite walkable. On the way, threading among other pedestrians, traffic and the horse-drawn carriages that came out on weekends, Adriana asked Val about his methods of developing photos.

"I have a darkroom—the door beside the stairway."

"Really? I wondered where that led." She thought about the dark Victorian house. "But then, there are plenty of rooms in your place that I haven't seen. Are most of them empty?"

"I fear so."

"You're going to work on the grounds first, then?"

He raised his brows. "The grounds?"

"You have all that dirt for landscaping," she reminded him, thinking of the boxes in the dining room.

"Ah, true." He nodded. "But I fear I have not started on the grounds, either."

"Are you going to plant flowers? It might be a little difficult with your allergy to the sun. You'll have to dig around at night. Would you like me to help you?"

"You are very kind, Adriana."

He smiled as they stopped at a streetlight. A carriage and a large white horse turned the corner. Lost in Val's gaze, Adriana didn't realize what was happening until she heard the squeals and snorting, the carriage driver's shouts.

Both she and Val backed away as the horse reared on its back legs, flailing its huge hooves.

"Down, hey, get down, Silver!" yelled the driver.

Other pedestrians also stepped back as the horse refused to settle. Squealing more loudly, it thrashed in its harness as if it wanted to bolt. The driver had his feet anchored and was pulling on the reins for all he was worth.

"Good heavens, the poor animal," said Adriana.

Eyes rolling, mouth frothing, the white horse reared again.

Val took hold of her, saying, "Let us go and quickly."

They fled, Adriana glancing over her shoulder when they were halfway down the block. The driver finally seemed to have calmed the animal.

Puzzled by the strange incident, she said, "The carriage horses are usually so gentle, not even afraid of traffic. And you're so good with animals—"

"Most animals. That one did not like my scent."

"Then it must not have been a female," she said archly.

That brought another smile to his usually serious face.

She glanced back a second time, noting the carriage and driver moving on...and a familiar-looking man ambling down the sidewalk, obviously following Val and her. When he realized Adriana saw him, he slipped into the doorway of a building.

Stone Drake.

Angry, she wondered what on earth her former boyfriend was doing. It was only ten-thirty—he was supposed to be working.

"Is something the matter?" asked Val.

"Uh, no."

He scowled, raising his head as if to sniff the wind. "If there are any more would-be abductors lurking about, they are going to be sorry."

Adriana said hurriedly, "It was nothing. I just thought I saw one of my neighbors." She pulled on his arm. "Let's go to the gallery. I can't wait to see your photographs."

She picked up the pace as they walked on, hoping Stone had the sense to disappear. Not that she feared he would tell Frank Nieman she was playing hooky instead of going to a doctor; Stone didn't care for authority figures. She simply disliked her ex-boyfriend and she knew Val considered him a rival. They didn't need an unpleasant encounter to ruin a nice evening.

The Night Gallery was an elegant hole in the wall run by a strange little man with a humpback. Val's work dominated one of the rooms. The other two featured paintings that had been used as cover art for dark fantasy and Gothic romance novels.

Adriana merely glanced at the paintings as Val led her to his photos.

"Do you recognize this neighborhood?" he asked, pointing to a photograph of a seedy bar with two men arguing beneath an eerily lit neon sign.

"Uptown."

Though it wasn't one of the shots he'd taken the night Adriana had accompanied him, thank God. She didn't want to be reminded of Eddie's services or Lilly's demise.

She moved away, Val talking about other parts of the city he'd prowled. Adriana liked his stage-door photos—he'd caught actors and dancers headed for home after productions were over.

"Nice lighting," she remarked. "And you've got a great sense of composition. These are really good."

"Thank you." Another smile.

She was even more fascinated by a striking group of photographs depicting panoramic views of Chicago—obviously taken from a great height.

"My heavens, how did you get that shot?" she mused as she stared at crisscrossing streets lined with lights and arced by beams from tiny cars.

"I have my ways."

"You rented a helicopter, right?"

Val merely shrugged as they moved to another photo, a skewed view of steel-and-glass canyons that cut through a forest of tall buildings.

"Wow, you must have had the pilot just about stand on his head for that one."

For some reason, the scene was very familiar to her.

Now he laughed softly.

"It almost makes me dizzy." *Dizzy.* As in her dream, Adriana suddenly recalled. "I had the wildest dream last night. "I think we were flying—"

"Flying, hmm?"

She tried to explain, "I mean, we were really flying. You know—without a plane."

"Not an unusual theme for dreams."

He sounded amused, and that bothered her. But before she had a chance to continue, the gallery's manager approached to speak to Val.

Afterward, she asked, "Did you make any sales?"

"One, perhaps."

"Are you disappointed?"

"Money is not the primary objective with my photographs."

"But surely you want other people to enjoy them."

"I want at least a few to see them. It makes me feel that I truly live."

What an odd statement. "Well, of course, you live." She added, "I guess I can understand, though. Any artist likes to be validated by interaction with other people. That's why I prefer working at the club over being a deejay on a radio program."

They were still talking about art and interaction when they left the gallery, and Adriana noticed that a poetry slam was being held next door at the Full Moon Café.

"Too bad there don't seem to be any empty tables." The place was packed. "The poetry is sometimes good." Though Adriana didn't particularly like the cruel tradition of the slam audience snapping their fingers at poems they didn't like, thereby humiliating the author.

"We shall listen for a while, if you wish," said Val. Even as he spoke, three people vacated a table inside the door.

"Well, that's certainly convenient."

He pulled out a chair for her, then sat himself. A waitress emerged from the throng to take their order for wine.

A young woman was reciting on the small stage at the other end of the establishment. "Your eyes possess me. Your lips obsess me. The night is wrapped in flesh-colored sheets...."

"How appropriate," Adriana murmured, glancing at Val.

But his attention was focused on the waitress, already delivering two glasses of red. "Are you Mr. Kadar? There's a phone call for you at the bar."

He frowned. "A phone call?"

"That's what the bartender said."

"Who would be calling me?" He looked none too happy.

"Maybe it's the manager at the Night Gallery," Adriana offered. "He could have seen us come in here."

Val rose. "I shall return in a moment."

She nodded and sipped some wine. The poet had moved on to another erotic selection about waking up in the morning, cradled in the arms of a lover.

Adriana had never awakened in Val's arms—at least, not in the morning. She decided she was going to ask him to stay overnight. If he was too allergic to the sun to go home then, she'd make them brunch and he could hang around all day. And if Jennifer came back, she'd get a chance to introduce them.

"Adriana?"

Pleasant images fled as she faced Stone Drake.

"What are you doing here?" she asked angrily. "I saw you following us earlier. Why aren't you at work?"

"I took off. What about you?" He came closer, placing a hand on the table and leaning over to meet her eye to eye. "Look, Adriana, you know I'm no saint, but I've got to warn you. There's terrible things going down... things I don't even know the half of. For one, that guy you're with is some weird dude. I don't even think he's human."

Her heartbeat picked up. "What on earth are you talking about?" If Irina had been spreading rumors, she was going to string the redhead up with one of her own glittery head scarves.

"I followed you last night, in another taxi. I saw that whole incident. Kadar ripped the door off the car and dragged the driver out with one hand. And, God... h-he had big sharp teeth and his eyes glowed in the dark!"

Cold chills climbed up and down her spine, especially because Stone truly looked freaked. "If this is some ploy to try to cause problems between me and Val, I'll—"

"I'm not trying to cause problems," Stone interjected, reaching out to grasp her shoulder for emphasis. "I'm telling the truth, babe. Your life is in danger. Take off. Get out of town. I'm heading for the airport tonight myself."

Which were the last words the man spoke before he was torn away and shoved with such force he slammed into a table behind him. It fell over, along with a chair containing a shocked customer. Glass crashed, people sprawled and a woman screamed.

Val towered over Stone, glaring. "How dare you touch her!"

"Leave me alone!" Downed, Stone nevertheless managed to scoot backward on his elbows. Blood streamed from his nose—he'd obviously hit it when he fell. "Leave me alone, please!" he croaked as Val leaned over and jerked him to his feet.

"Lowborn cur!" Val shook him. "You told them to say I had a phone call, didn't you? So you could get your hands on Adriana!"

"Val!" In shock, Adriana jumped up and rushed into the fray. "Please! Don't hurt anyone!"

At least her grasp on Val's arm made him release Stone, who stumbled backward.

But then Val turned on her, his fiery gaze nearly making her want to cower. "You protect this thief again?"

"Hey, man, I've got her mixes in the car," said Stone, still backing away, wiping blood from his nose on a shirtsleeve. "She's welcome to them."

"I don't care about the mixes!" cried Adriana. "They aren't that important. I just don't want to see anyone hurt!"

Val didn't seem reassured. "You mean you do not wish to see your ex-lover hurt, don't you?"

"You don't understand," said Adriana, glancing around at the interested crowd. She lowered her voice. "And this is not the place to talk." They were the center of attention, and surely the police were being called.

Stone had already split. She urged, "Let's get out of here."

Even passersby had gathered outside the place, but the gathering parted before Val. Adriana followed him closely, and they found a shadowy gangway. Just in time. Adriana glanced back and spotted blazing blue lights. Police cars had descended on the café.

They hurried along, coming out into a dark alley. Adriana held her tongue until they'd left the alley behind and crossed a street to blend into a knot of people emerging from a movie theater.

Then she complained breathlessly, "You can't act this way. It's not civilized. And it...it scares me. You know that. I've told you."

Tight-lipped, Val said nothing.

"I don't care about Stone," she insisted. "I don't even like him."

"Then why do you come to his defense?"

"Just because I dislike someone doesn't mean I want to see him picked up and thrown across a room." She added accusingly, "And if you think so, then we don't belong together."

Again, Val didn't respond. Silently, he stalked past the moviegoers and headed for Michigan Avenue. They were only a couple of blocks from Adriana's building. Val's expression was stern and cold as he turned in the direction of Oak Street. He only stopped when they reached the open intersection from which the lake was visible.

"I believe you are correct, Adriana," he said finally. "We do not belong together. I am too old-fashioned, too jealous...yet too principled. I will not take you against your will, but I cannot tolerate allowing you free choice."

"What are you talking about with this 'taking me' business? Some courtship rite from Hungary?"

He didn't answer directly. "This will not work between us. I have made a serious mistake."

"Or else you can learn to deal with your insecurity. We need to have a long discussion."

"A discussion will change nothing." He stepped away.

She couldn't believe him! "Where do you think you're going?"

"To hell . . . for all I care, if I cannot have you." And he took off.

"Val!" She couldn't believe it! "How many times do I have to tell you that Stone means nothing—"

But he was already a quarter of the way down the block. She followed, running to catch up, only to find he'd disappeared by the time she reached the corner. As usual, when he wanted to vanish, he did so easily.

She sighed, the fatigue she'd felt before he'd arrived that night seeming to creep right back up on her. Too drained to do a good job at being angry, she made her way back to her building, knowing she could do little more than fall into bed.

She only hoped she could sleep.

Later that night, Stone Drake left Adriana's CDs with the doorman in the superstitious hope that giving them back would help alleviate his troubles. Everything had started going wrong right after he'd approached her about them, the first evening he'd started working at After Dark.

Well, that gig was gone, as well as his paycheck. He'd left without so much as punching out and he didn't intend to give the place a forwarding address.

He'd been telling Adriana the truth about getting out of town. If she didn't want to listen, it was her funeral, but he didn't intend to stick around and deal with heavy hitters like Miklos Rakosi... or whatever the hell Valentin Kadar was.

Quickly scanning the street when he came back outside, he headed for his car. At this time of the night, it would only take a half hour to get to the airport.

But before Stone reached his vehicle, a dark figure quietly detached itself from the shadow of a parked van, placing itself directly in his path. A man wearing a broad-brimmed hat and a coat with a cape about the shoulders.

Recognizing him, Stone froze. "You!"

But he stood there only a moment. Then, adrenaline flowing, he took off at a dead run, blindly leaping the barriers of Lake Shore Drive and careening across the highway, all eight lanes. A passing driver hit the brakes.

On the other side, Stone jumped yet another barrier, falling, tumbling down onto the beach. The thud behind him meant his pursuer was still following.

Stone ran on, his feet kicking up sand. Younger than his pursuer, he could surely outdistance the man.

He was wrong.

With tremendous leaps, the man in the caped coat was soon breathing down his neck. And a strong hand slammed him so hard in the back, Stone fell, sprawling.

"No!" he screamed, mouth full of sand.

Then he could only gurgle as a viselike grip pinned him and he realized the relentless, savage visage looming over him would be the last thing he ever saw....

CHAPTER TWELVE

Adriana found herself able to sleep, despite her unhappiness and agitation. Though she tossed and turned with the most restless, bizarre, yet realistic-seeming dreams. Once she envisioned her lover hovering outside her bedroom window...then started as she realized her eyes were wide open.

"Val?"

Even as she spoke, the night sky seemed to shift and she was staring straight into the dark, though she swore she caught sight of a pale scarf fluttering just beyond the window frame.

But Valentin Kadar couldn't be up here, looking in her sixth-floor window—not unless he could fly.

Thinking of the photos that could only have been taken from midair, goose bumps rising on her arms and neck, Adriana threw back the covers and went to investigate. As expected, the night outside was quiet but for occasional cars passing on the drive below. The moon glowed clear and white in the sky, though a mist hung low over the lake.

Her imagination must be running away with her, Adriana decided. Or else she was losing her mind.

She had to settle down. Thinking to fix herself some herbal tea that might bring on a deeper sleep, she headed for the kitchen at the rear of the apartment, not bothering to switch on any lights. With open curtains and blinds, a combination of city illumination and a bright moon made it easy enough to see.

Though she almost stumbled when Phantom mewed and weaved in and out between her legs. It didn't help when the cat decided to play with the edge of her long nightgown.

"Bad kitty," she said, not really meaning it. "So you escaped. But Jens isn't here to insist I lock you up again."

In the kitchen, which was lit by a fancy night-light, she poured the cat a small saucer of milk and petted her before running water into the teakettle. Waiting for the kettle to fill, she opened a cabinet door to get a mug, then the silverware drawer to choose a spoon.

As she did so, a hissing sound startled her. The cat! Phantom faced the back door, her fur standing on end. And her hiss turned into a low growl that ran shivers up and down Adriana's spine.

"What on earth?"

The door opened to a fire escape with a lower twelve-foot tier that didn't reach the ground. But after everything that had happened to her lately, Adriana couldn't help feeling spooked. Without thinking, she grabbed a butcher knife from the silverware drawer and switched off the water.

Phantom's growl turned into a warning yowl as Adriana advanced to the door.

"Go away, kitty," she told the cat, stamping her foot. "Hide!"

The cat took off as, heart pounding in her ears, Adriana prepared to do battle. The top of the door was latticed glass and she slid along the wall, craning her neck to look. A dark figure stood against the fire-escape railing, staring directly toward her. She was shrouded in shadow but somehow she knew he could see her.

Something pale fluttered.... A scarf?

"Val?"

With trembling hands, she laid aside the knife, quickly undoing the dead bolt and the other two locks on the door. It swung open and Val came inside to slide his arms about her.

"Forgive me," he whispered. "It seems that I cannot leave you, after all."

She reveled in his touch, felt the imprint of each of his fingers through the delicate fabric of the nightgown. "You don't have to ask for my forgiveness. I never asked you to go."

Only to control his temper. But maybe that was possible if he could allow himself to become more sure of her. And maybe that just took a while with a passionate, old-world Hungarian.

To prove her devotion, she slipped her arms about his neck and kissed him as if this were to be their last meeting on earth. He responded with equal fervor, groaning as their tongues danced, as she rocked her hips against him. He picked her up, and she wrapped her legs about his waist.

"Your bedroom...where is it?" he whispered, easily carrying her down the hallway.

She raised her head to gesture and he entered her door. A little hiss beneath the bed meant Phantom was hiding there.

"Poor kitty, she's afraid of you."

"Don't worry. We shall make friends. Cats like me."

And then Adriana was aware of nothing but Val—his lips, his hands, the hardness of his body. Throwing his own clothing aside, he drew her nightgown over her head and joined them completely. Adriana writhed, her head thrashing from side to side as he brought her to ecstasy. But she wanted sweeter still and arched her neck.

He hesitated, murmuring, "This could be dangerous for you."

"Dangerous?"

She pressed her throat against his lips and he took what she had asked him to.

The night swam, danced. Stars wheeled and the moon flew. Clinging to Val, the only solid entity in a shifting universe, Adriana shuddered over and over...until she lost consciousness....

The room was gray when she awakened later and realized Val had risen to dress. "Going so soon? Don't you want to stay for breakfast?"

"I am already satiated."

"You didn't eat that much at dinner."

"I need to return to my house. And you need rest from my company."

She noticed the little creature winding herself about his feet. Val picked up the cat.

"You made friends with Phantom."

"I told you we would get along." He came to the bed, petting the purring cat before settling her beside the pillow. "Little Phantom is quite charming...like her mistress."

Adriana lay back and took hold of his lapels, pulling him down. She pouted provocatively. "Are you sure you have to go?"

"Unfortunately, yes." He kissed her, then pulled back.

Which was when she noticed the dark stain on his jacket. "What's that?"

"Blood. From Stone Drake's nose."

"Oh." She'd forgotten about the whole unpleasant incident.

"Take care of yourself, Adriana. Sleep in and have some red meat with your meals. You won't feel so dizzy or weak."

"Sleep I can understand, but meat?"

"Seriously," he said. "Even a small amount will help. . . until you make your final choice."

"Choice?" She gave him a perplexed look.

"You will need to see everything clearly, first."

"What the heck are you talking about?" Whether she should be a meat eater or a vegetarian?

He was slipping out the door. "Farewell, my lovely one."

She started to rise and follow, then figured it was no use.

Besides, she could rest easy, knowing she and Val had made up. There would be plenty of time to discuss his mysterious, strange ways in the nights to come.

Red meat. Val had been correct about it giving her energy, Adriana thought as she swept out of her building to take a taxi to work that evening. Having found some filet mignon in the freezer, she'd defrosted it and fixed herself a hearty late-afternoon brunch of steak, omelet and salad. Afterward, she'd called Frank to say she'd be working, that she felt great.

She entered the club smiling, only to find a lot of somber faces and whisperings among the other employees.

"What's the matter?" she asked, approaching Frank.

He stood at the bar with Peter. "Haven't you heard, darling? There's been yet another murder."

Gazing at her meaningfully, Peter added, "And this time it was real close to home—Stone Drake."

Her throat constricted. "Stone?"

"I'm very surprised you heard nothing about this," said Frank. "He took off last night, didn't even punch out. Later, his body was discovered on Oak Street Beach—right below your building. The police said a motorist on the drive spotted a struggle between two men and reported it on his car phone. They are searching for the murderer, who is still at large."

In her mind's eye, she saw Val throwing Stone into the table at the café.

"This time all the blood wasn't drained so neat and nice out of the body, though." Peter grimaced. "It was splattered all over the place."

Adriana recalled the dark stain on Val's jacket. He'd admitted it was Stone's blood. But surely he wouldn't have been so quick to explain, so blithe, if he'd just finished murdering the man. Would he?

Even though he was fiercely jealous?

Her stomach knotted and her knees grew weak.

"Are you sure you want to stay tonight?" Frank asked her. "I've already canceled the radio broadcast. I tried to explain that when you phoned, but you didn't give me the chance."

Her mind spun, but she knew she didn't want to go home. "I'll work. I'd like to be around people."

Rather than be alone. The condo might very well be empty—from time to time, Jennifer spent an entire weekend with Todd.

And, at the moment, Adriana had no intention of conjuring up Val. Surely he wouldn't, couldn't, have come back to her last night because he'd solved his problem with jealousy... by eliminating his rival.

She refused to think so, though the entire situation was giving her the creeps.

Later, working in the sound booth, the shock finally wearing off, she started feeling sad for Stone himself. He'd been a problematic person, but he hadn't deserved to be murdered.

With his blood splattered all over....

Adriana shivered as the CD she'd been playing came to an end. "And now we have a live band—Evanescence—to play for you."

She took off her earphones and left the booth, ambling through the crowd and into the bar. There Irina spotted her and started hurrying up the card reading she was doing, no doubt wanting to talk.

Great. But Adriana felt too demoralized to hide from her friend. Or anyone. She ordered a tonic and lime from Peter and wondered when Detective Panchella would be in to see her again.

As expected, Irina headed directly for the bar when she was finished with her customer. "You look a little better than you did last night, but you're still too pale."

"I feel a lot better."

"Even though Stone was killed?"

"I'm upset about that, of course. How could you think I wouldn't be?" She explained, "I meant I feel better physically."

"Val didn't like Stone, did he?"

Adriana hedged, "Val is very protective in an old-fashioned way. He felt Stone had wronged me."

"Hmmph." Irina opened her purse, withdrawing a piece of paper. "Mr. Kadar is old-fashioned, all right, and he's got about seven hundred reasons why."

"Seven hundred?"

"Years." Irina unfolded the piece of paper. A photocopy. "Take a look at this—it's a portrait of that Hungarian nobleman we were talking about—the Kadar."

Adriana felt compelled to look, moving the photocopy beneath one of the lights that hung over the bar. A somber visage stared out at her, a man with high cheekbones, a straight nose and a wide, sensual mouth. He seemed to be dressed in a tunic of some sort and had shoulder-length dark hair, but she had to admit the portrait resembled Val enough to give her a chill.

But some photocopied picture couldn't make her believe in superstition. She was far more concerned that Val might be a murderer than a vampire. Not that she could share her horrible doubts with anyone, including Irina.

She objected, "I've taken an art-history course. They didn't do portraits like this in the thirteenth century."

"It's from the sixteenth century. Legend has it that the Kadar was already three hundred years old then."

"Uh-huh. Legend." Adriana handed the photocopy back.

"That's not all. A chemist tested that herb mixture."

"The herbs?" Adriana frowned. "The ones you scooped up from the bar? There wasn't very much."

"Enough to analyze. The mixture contains crushed carrot seeds, flax seeds, millet, mustard, paprika and some sort of ground tree bark."

"So?"

"According to my aunt, that's a classic mix for curbing vampirism." Irina paid no attention to Adriana's sigh. "But herbs only curb the syndrome, not cure it. He would still have the power to appear and disappear at will, superhuman strength."

Adriana became alert. "Superhuman strength?"

"Not to mention that vampires can fly."

"Fly?" Her dream coming back in great clarity, she nearly choked on a swallow of tonic water.

"He wouldn't have to take a bat form, of course. He could just zap around here and there when he wanted to." Irina leaned closer, concern in her expression. "I can tell you're freaked. Seen him hovering around your windows lately?"

Adriana refused to let legend overwhelm logic. "I simply can't believe in vampires, Irina. If I did, I'd also have to believe in everything else—sorcerers, werewolves, fairies, leprechauns."

Now it was Irina's turn to say, "So?"

"You actually accept such beings as reality?"

Irina looked perfectly solemn. "I accept them as possibilities. No one can prove they don't exist."

"But no one can prove they do, either." Adriana leaned against the bar. "Valentin Kadar is a very unusual man, but that doesn't mean he's supernatural. And he's honorable and decent." At least, most of the time. "He can be very kind," she stated, in a way trying to reassure herself. "He gives money to the homeless and the lost and he takes in stray animals."

"As far as the homeless are concerned, he's either paying them as spies or showing off for you. And animals...well, vampires can often hold simpler life-forms in their thrall. Especially night creatures like cats and owls and bats."

Cats and owls. Okay. "What about dogs?"

"They use them as watch animals. A dog guards his master's residence while he sleeps." Irina went on,

"Actually, vampires are rather animalistic themselves. They can charm just about any kind of beast except a white horse."

"A horse?" With a thrill, Adriana thought of the carriage steed the night before.

"White horses can detect the undead. In Europe, people used to lead them across cemeteries when they suspected a vampire was hanging out in a grave or crypt." Irina added, "Ah-hah. Your eyes are really big. I know the stuff I'm saying is getting to you."

She could only shake her head. "I feel like I'm living in some sort of dream." Or nightmare, actually.

"I can imagine. You didn't really break up with Val, did you? He's been hypnotizing you, charming you, making love...and taking blood when he gets the chance. You've got your hair pulled forward, but I noticed the mark on your throat."

Adriana placed her hand there protectively. The wound throbbed slightly. Val *had* bitten her.

"What does it feel like?" Irina asked. "The process must be pleasurable or victims like you wouldn't get into it."

Pleasurable wasn't the word for the way Val's passionate ministrations made her feel. But Adriana didn't intend to admit anything to Irina, who had not only gotten on her nerves but was truly frightening her.

She eased herself off the stool. "Look, I appreciate your trying to warn me about all this, but if I have some concerns about Val, it's not because I believe he's a vampire."

"You think he's just a straight killer."

Irina certainly had good instincts. But Adriana objected, "Nothing has been proven." And she suddenly remembered the botched abduction two nights ago.

"Furthermore, there's somebody else involved in this whole mess because some crazy guy tried to haul me off in a stolen taxi on Thursday."

"Yeah?"

She could tell Irina was surprised. "I didn't get the chance to tell you about it because I was sick on Friday night. Val obviously has an enemy who's doing these killings and is trying to frame him."

Which made her feel better. All the other details Irina had mentioned in trying to prove her point simply had to be a set of very bizarre circumstances.

But Irina's expression had become worried. "Now I see. There's probably a pack of vampires and they're having a war!"

"Vampires!" Upset all over again, Adriana wanted to tear her hair. "I've heard enough about this subject—I've told you that before." She made one last threat before heading back toward the dance floor. "Don't bring it up again or I'm not even going to talk to you!"

But in the isolation of the sound booth, playing CDs throughout the remainder of the night, she couldn't help brooding on many, many things. Stone claiming Val had had big teeth and glowing eyes. The snarling sounds and the torn taxi door. Val's strength—the way he could pick up grown men and throw them around. The rearing white carriage horse.

And the list went on. Val's seeming ability to appear and disappear. The dreams of flying. Her vision of his hovering near her bedroom window.

The way he drew her to him, made her pulse thrum. The sublime ecstasy he created whenever they made love.

Ecstasy. Adriana touched her throat with a trembling hand, appalled because, at the moment, legend and superstition actually seemed to make sense.

Miklos Rakosi laid out his most desperate plan, the only one that made any sense. There would be no more anonymous phone calls to the police, useless after the murder of Stone Drake. He would have to depend on his own cunning to rid himself of Kadar.

In the wee hours, he called Zeke and another burly thug into the main cabin of the *Buckthorn.*

"Go get the woman tomorrow morning and bring her back to the boat."

"How early?" asked Zeke.

"Six or seven. As soon as the sun rises above the horizon."

"Alive or dead?" inquired the other thug, a man who liked to act macho.

"Alive, of course. Kadar won't appear otherwise."

"How would he know?"

"He will know, believe me." Not that a fool like this would understand, unless he'd heard gossip from those who'd seen Kadar interrupt the craps game. Rakosi had tried his best to play that down but he knew that many of his employees, hardened men, were frightened. "Be careful. There is a doorman to avoid." He handed Zeke, a former thief and the more intelligent of the two men, the piece of paper. "Here is the message you are to give her sister." He had written it out carefully, in case neither man got it straight.

The sister would take action.

And the last chapter on the medallion would be written.

After waving the men away, Rakosi sat back, fingering and admiring his treasure. The only inheritance he would ever receive from a father who hadn't looked backward and a harlot of a mother who'd wanted a passing thrill. She'd abandoned her son on some peasant farmer's doorstep. It had taken him years to find out who and what he truly was.

Then he'd had to risk life and soul to gain the legacy due him. The medallion he'd stolen wasn't much to look at, merely ancient iron and bloodstones. But the power it gave...

Rakosi would fight to the death to keep it.

Though he hoped he wouldn't have to. That's why he was sending his men to do the initial legwork while he rested and conserved his energy, readying himself for the final confrontation beneath a blazing sun.

CHAPTER THIRTEEN

Adriana didn't want to go home alone. She didn't want to face any shadows, dark windows or dreams tonight by herself.

Yet she avoided Irina and the other employees when her final shift was over. After Frank said he didn't mind if she used his phone for a private call or two, she quickly slipped up to his office, eyes darting about.

Murder and mayhem.

Spooked and paranoid, she longed to be with someone she could trust, someone who had her feet on the ground, someone she'd known all her life. Jennifer had a car and, if she pleaded, her sister would surely pick her up.

She couldn't help the hour. She would have called earlier if her head had been clear. Punching in numbers, she counted the rings before Jennifer's answering machine kicked in.

When the message had finished, she spoke anxiously, "Jens, are you there? Grab the phone, will you? I need you to drive over to the club and get me. Come on, Jens."

No one answered. Damn! Since Jennifer never turned off her phone, this meant that her sister had stayed another night at her fiancé's or was too deeply asleep to respond. She slammed the receiver down, gave the machine a little time to rewind, then called again. The message only played a second time.

"Double damn!"

Riffling in her purse, she drew out her little address book and tried Todd this time. She wanted to scream when *his* answering machine picked up. Where was everyone when she needed them? Taking a deep breath, she tried three more calls. One to her own machine—which held no messages—the second to Jennifer's number, the last to Todd's again. Only machines were responding at this hour.

She was almost thinking of calling her parents, who now lived in Florida, when she realized such action would only upset them and do her absolutely no good. She would simply have to take care of herself, make her own decisions. Inhaling a deep, calming breath, she tried to settle down, wondering if she should drop by the police station to stay the rest of the night.

But what if Irina's theories were as half-cocked as anyone with a rational mind would doubtlessly think they were?

What if Val were innocent of any wrongdoing?

What if he weren't?

What if he truly did have . . . special powers?

In case her lover could sense her moods and desires, she concentrated, speaking into the empty space of the room, "Stay away from me, Valentin Kadar. I don't need you. I don't want you and you'd better not show your face anywhere near me again!"

She almost added that she'd be carrying a sharpened stake and wearing a garlic necklace just to make sure, when the ridiculousness of the whole situation struck her. Starting out with a giggle, she was soon chortling, then laughing aloud before choking up with unshed tears.

This wouldn't do! Taking a deep breath, she slammed her fist down on the desk. "I won't get hysterical! I won't! I can take care of myself."

In fact, a plan had already formed in her mind. With only a few hours left until dawn, she'd simply gird her loins and take a taxi to the all-night steak-and-egger in her neighborhood. The place was always busy on weekends—Val or his enemies couldn't come and sweep her away without someone noticing.

Besides, she was hungry. Not having eaten since the meal she'd fixed before work, she'd treat herself to a juicy burger while she read the Sunday papers and waited for the sun to rise.

Seven-thirty.

Adriana glanced at her watch again, deciding it was finally safe enough to walk home. Having finished reading every section of the *Chicago Tribune* and the *Sun-Times,* having worked every crossword and puzzle, she'd nevertheless spent more time than she wanted staring into the night-dark glass of the diner and hoping she wouldn't glimpse anything scary on the other side.

She also hoped she hadn't made a mistake by staying out at all. But she was certain Jennifer hadn't returned to the condo. She'd made several calls an hour, until her sister's answering machine had shut down.

And Phantom was surely safe. The cat would hide if any strangers came knocking at the door.

Still, guilt made Adriana hurry after she'd paid her bill.

The morning was glorious. A bright sun had risen above the lake, gilding the turquoise water with gold. A lover of the night, Adriana grudgingly admitted that today the sunlight made her fears seem less ominous.

Not that there hadn't been murders. And not that Val wasn't strange. But that didn't mean there wasn't a logical explanation for his actions or that he wasn't correct in claiming that some horrible person was killing people and, for some reason, trying to blame it on him.

Adriana assured herself she'd think about everything later, after she'd gotten some sleep.

When she entered her building, the first thing she noticed was Henry dozing. No wonder—the poor man must work fifteen-hour shifts and rarely seemed to take any days off.

She approached his desk. "Henry?"

He grunted, started. "Huh?"

"Have you seen my sister, Jennifer, around? Do you know if she's home?"

"Jennifer Thorn? Yeah, she came in a minute ago." He gazed at his watch, seemingly uncomfortable. "Er, I mean, I guess it was an hour ago. She asked me to escort her upstairs."

"Really?" Then Jennifer must have stayed somewhere else for the night. And must have been frightened for some reason. She chewed her lip, concerned. "Is the apartment all right?"

"A'course it's all right." He scowled. "Somebody trying to scare you girls?"

"You heard about the murders in this neighborhood."

"Sure, but nothing like that is going to happen here, not with me on the job."

As long as he didn't sleep too soundly, that is.

Adriana started to walk away, heading for the elevator, when Henry called after her, "I gave your sister that bag some guy left for you on Friday."

"A bag?" What on earth could that be?

Henry looked a bit uncomfortable again. "You left so fast yesterday, I forgot to give it to you."

"That's all right."

Adriana was simply grateful that Jennifer was safe and sound. On the sixth floor, she walked the carpeted, quiet hallway and inserted her key in the door.

Inside, the entryway was equally quiet, though she spotted a brown-paper shopping bag on the chair beside the coat closet, the delivery Henry must have been referring to. Curious, she peered inside, stunned to see more than a dozen labeled CDs, the mixes Stone had stolen from her.

My God, did that mean he'd delivered them the very night he'd been killed? Then encountered Val afterward?

Chilled, shaken all over again, she paced down the hallway and called, "Jens? I got the bag you carried up."

Had it freaked Jennifer, too? Her sister knew that Stone had possessed the mixes and she must have heard or read about Stone's murder somewhere. Maybe the latter was the reason she hadn't come home last night, because she'd been scared.

"Jens?" Adriana called again, glancing into her sister's bedroom, then around the huge living room. A cool breeze wafted from the rear of the apartment. "Jens, where are you?"

The only answer was a plaintive meow from her own bedroom...the door to which she was certain she'd closed.

Now it was open.

"Phantom." She peeked in, ready to scoop up the little black cat. She was puzzled when her pet meowed again, from beneath the bed. Stooping, she could see only a crouched form and two limpid green eyes. "Did you get scared again, baby?" She reached in, felt Phantom all over. The animal was fine.

The cat rubbed against her hand but remained tense. Why? Adriana was beginning to have a creepy feeling. The breeze was definitely growing stronger.

"Jens?"

She started to walk, then broke into a half run for the kitchen...where the breeze blew in the door leading to the fire escape. It gaped wide open, the locks broken!

Her heart pounded. "Jens!"

My God, and the kitchen was a mess! A chair and the small table of Jennifer's breakfast set had been overturned. Nearby, a cup lay smashed on the floor in a puddle of coffee, mixed with the remains of the kitchen phone. It had been pulled from the wall, leaving a ragged hole.

"Where are you, Jens?" she cried, even knowing her sister was gone.

Terror swept through her, freezing her blood to ice. Desperate, she ran out onto the fire escape, recalling Val standing out there two nights ago.

But no one was here now. Nothing moved below in the alley.

Filled with guilt, she rushed back into the apartment. "It's all my fault!"

She should have come home last night despite her misgivings so that Val or whoever had invaded the apartment this morning wouldn't have found Jennifer alone.

Breath shallow, eyes darting, she tried to figure out what to do. Call Henry?

No, the police!

But the phones weren't working. Praying her own line had been left untouched, she started back for her bedroom. That's when she noticed the butcher knife sticking out of a chopping board on the counter, the blade securing a piece of paper.

She halted, lunged for the counter, pulling the knife free. The message on the paper was carefully printed.

> Adriana Thorn is being held on my boat. If you want her to live beyond noon, you will contact Valentin Kadar instead of the police. I say noon—do not waste time!

Val's address was written out, as if the person who'd been expected to read the note wouldn't know where to find him. Adriana's mind spun, registering the truth. Jennifer had been kidnapped, though the victim was supposed to have been *her*.

Poor, innocent Jens!

Poor sister who walked the safe daylight, who never looked twice at dangerous, dark men. For, even if he hadn't done this deed, Valentin Kadar was involved up to his eyeballs.

And now he was going to have to come to Jennifer's rescue.

Knowing what she had to do, Adriana slammed the fire-escape door closed, pushed a chair against it, then ran to get the extra cash she had hidden in a shoebox in her closet. Stuffing the bills in her purse, she sprinted for the elevator and, downstairs, ran straight past a snoozing Henry.

There weren't any taxis in sight on Oak Street, so she raced for Michigan Avenue. When the first vehicle appeared, she jumped out in front to flag it down, ignoring the irate driver's protests as she scrambled inside.

Thrusting several bills at the driver, she gave Val's address, then gestured toward the drive. "Step on it!"

"I don't want to get a ticket, lady."

She opened her purse and extracted more money. "Here. And there's more where that came from. Now get this heap moving. This is a life-and-death situation!"

The man must have believed her, because he floored the accelerator, sending the vehicle shooting out onto the outer drive. Lake Michigan sped by on one side, Lincoln Park on the other. Adriana watched the hand of the odometer climb from thirty to sixty-five. At the Lawrence exit, the driver slowed, but not enough to stop the vehicle from nearly making a wheelie as it zoomed up a ramp and made a sharp turn onto the street.

They sped down Lawrence until Adriana ordered, "Take a right."

Another wheelie, two blocks, and the decaying Victorian mansion came into sight.

"Stop!" she yelled, bringing the driver to a squealing halt. "And wait right here, I'm coming back."

Charging out of the taxi, she ran for the mansion, hoping the door would open before her like it had before. She mounted the steps expectantly, grasped the doorknob, turned it.

No luck. The door didn't budge. "Damn!"

Furthermore, loud, furious barking erupted from inside. At least that should wake Val. To add more noise, Adriana pounded on the wooden panels so hard, her fists stung.

"Val!"

No answer. More barking and the thud of the dog's body as he threw himself against the door from the inside. My God, the sweet-natured animal must turn into a raving beast when he was on sentry duty.

A dog guards his master's residence while he sleeps.

But Adriana refused to think about Irina's folklore. Either Val wasn't home—which she prayed wasn't the case—or he was an incredibly sound sleeper. She'd simply have to break in.

She chose the low window that opened off the porch. The boards that had once covered it were rotten and sagging. Grunting, she managed to tear one off. Then she wielded it like a baseball bat, smashing the latticed glass beneath.

Crash. Tinkle.

Surely Val would hear that. But he wasn't around when she squeezed through the opening she'd made, tearing her long skirt. The black Lab growled, advancing toward her with the hair on his neck standing on end, his lips drawn into a snarl.

Geez. But she refused to be afraid, crooning softly, "Hey, doggie, you know me. I've been here before." She held out a hand, hoping it wouldn't be bitten. "Hey, you know my scent."

The animal sniffed her suspiciously, but seemed to settle down. At least he quit snarling.

"Nice doggie," she chanted, moving slowly but purposefully toward the stairway. "I won't hurt you or your master, either."

The dog didn't follow her upstairs. The door to Val's bedroom was closed but not locked, so she swung it open and tried to make out the bed in the near darkness.

She remembered the candles that were always sitting around and found one by touch. She also located a box of matches on the dresser. A tiny flame flared as she lit the candle, then carried it to the four-poster. Val lay there on his back, fully dressed in pants and smoking jacket. But he seemed so still, so unmoving... almost as if he were dead.

"Val!" She touched him, flinching when his flesh seemed cold. She would swear he wasn't breathing. "Val, please be okay! Dear God!"

She flinched again when his eyelids suddenly opened to reveal fierce, fiery gold orbs. His gaze burned like a laser, strong enough to chew a hole through her.

But she wouldn't, couldn't, be swayed from her purpose. "Please help me, Val!" she cried, nearly sobbing. "Someone's kidnapped Jennifer and he's going to kill her unless you come to his boat!"

Having been roused from deepest sleep, Val had a difficult time focusing. All he knew was that the woman he adored was leaning over his bed, babbling hysterically. He frowned. "Jennifer?"

"My sister. Someone broke down the back door this morning and took her. He thought she was me!"

Another abduction. This one successful. Thinking of Rakosi as his wits returned, angry at the very insolence of the man, he sat up and gazed about. "What time is it?"

"I don't know—eight-thirty or nine."

"A.M.?"

"Yes, morning." Her expression and tone were suffused with worry, grief. She trembled, repressing a sob. "I love Jennifer! I'd rather die myself than have anything happen to her!"

Sympathetic, Val pushed aside the time problem as he rose to take her in his arms. "My poor, sweet Adriana."

She sobbed for real, tears streaming out of her beautiful gray eyes. For a moment or two, she clung to him. Then she drew back, again fighting to keep her emotions in control.

"We have to go! There's no time to waste. We've only got until noon!"

The full fire of the sun. But any sort of daylight was deadly. "Rakosi is a crafty one."

"Rakosi?"

"The abductor." He went to his closet, changed jackets, then slung on his voluminous caped raincoat and a broad-brimmed hat from the shelf above. "I am not at my best at this time of the day." And he would be placing himself in mortal danger. "But I will save your sister, if it is the last thing I do on this earth. I, too, value family loyalty."

When he'd donned the coat, she helped him wrap a long scarf to raise the collar about his face.

"You really are terribly allergic, aren't you?"

"I must be careful." He drew on gloves, then headed for the door with her.

Downstairs, facing the day, he shuddered and shrank into his coverings. But he hurried as Adriana led him to a waiting taxi. The driver asked for directions.

Adriana turned to Val. "Where's the boat?"

"I assumed you knew."

She looked terribly anxious. "The note only said that Jennifer was being held on a boat. It didn't give an address."

"Damnation." Rakosi had definitely thought he'd captured Adriana . . . whom Val would have been able to find by sense alone. And, because of her danger, he would have been at the boat by now, even facing the sun.

"How are we going to find her?" Adriana worried.

"Do not worry, we shall. Drive downtown to the Chicago River," he told the driver, "while we do some guessing."

The man took off, muttering, and Adriana looked scared.

"Come closer," Val told her, slipping an arm about her shoulders. "Think on your sister with all your heart and soul. Envision her, call to her. She is of your blood." He lowered his voice, "We will have to sense her through our connection."

Their bond. His love.

Love? Yes. Adriana was the one.

If her beautiful visage were to be the last thing he ever saw, if he could grant her soft heart's dearest wish, he could leave this world, face judgment in the next one, at peace.

Adriana didn't care what sort of mumbo jumbo Val was using to locate Jennifer. She only prayed the method would work.

She became concerned when the taxi drove beside the river, up and down Wacker Drive for a while. She peered into the gap left between Val's hat and upturned collar, able to see only his eyes. "Are you sure the boat is around here?"

"It was here...not long ago." He grasped her more tightly. "But now it has moved farther north."

"The north branch?" She told the driver, "Take Clybourn."

The vehicle left the downtown area, soon entering the diagonal byway that had once cut through a heavily industrialized area. Now many former factories stood empty while fancy town houses and lofts were being built on nearby side streets.

Adriana closed her eyes, imagining Jennifer, asking Val, "Are the, uh, vibrations any stronger?"

"Thankfully, yes." He gestured west, in the direction of an abandoned-looking, fenced concrete lot. "Over there."

"Take a left," Adriana told the taxi driver.

The man grumbled, but he turned the vehicle through the open gate and sped across the lot's expanse. The car bounced over crisscrossing, unused railroad tracks.

Adriana went back to visualizing her sister until Val said, "Here. Right here. I feel her."

"Stop!" ordered Adriana, her hopes rising as she sighted the river...and a large white boat.

Val did have psychic powers!

After he paid the taxi, the vehicle took off.

They were on their own and she had no idea of who or what they faced. As they approached the boat, she saw its name stenciled on the prow, the *Buckthorn.* And she heard raucous laughter. A big scruffy man with thick eyebrows stood on the deck, near the ramp connecting it to the shore. She recognized him from Irina's photos.

"Miklos Rakosi," hissed Val.

Adriana didn't care what the man's name was, couldn't stop her temper from surging. "You idiot!"

she screamed at Rakosi as they came closer. "You have the wrong woman! I'm Adriana Thorn!" Which he would have known by visiting the club. She demanded, "Where's my sister?"

The big man only sneered. "I realized the oafs had made a mistake when they brought in my hostage." He indicated Val. "Luckily, it made no difference to my dear cousin. He is here to work out our differences beneath the bright sun."

Cousin?

"I prefer shade," said Val. "We will go inside."

Rakosi growled, "I think not—"

He was cut off when Val mounted the ramp with lightning speed. He shoved Rakosi backward with such force, the man's hurtling body knocked the boat's door right off its hinges. Rakosi fell inside the cabin, Val plunging after with a roar.

Her heart in her throat, Adriana followed as fast as she could, not caring what dangers she faced. Thuds and crashing within the cabin meant Val and Rakosi were fighting.

Fighting was hardly the word. She stood in the doorway, transfixed as the two men rolled and punched, snarling with fury, throwing each other into walls and built-in furniture. Wood cracked and shredded. Val's hat flew off, flying toward her.

Adriana stooped to pick it up...when a big hand reached out and grabbed her in a bruising grip. She cried out as she was whipped about to face a gun. There'd been two more men in the large cabin, hiding inside the door. Adriana stared down the barrel of the automatic, thinking she'd been stupid if she'd thought the kidnappers wouldn't be armed. But she hadn't thought and didn't know what she could have done about it, anyway.

Both the man who held her, a swarthy type, and his companion looked extremely uptight, as if they wanted to leave the scene of the horrendous battle.

Val bellowed and threw himself on top of Rakosi, who fought back by trying to choke him.

The swarthy gunman asked, "Hey, Zeke, think shooting the guy's girlfriend will do any good?"

Zeke glanced nervously at the combatants. "He don't seem to be payin' much attention."

But Val did notice, smacking Rakosi's head against the floor several times until the man lay still, rising swiftly to fly at the gunman. He grasped the man's wrist, the bones cracking. "Take your hands from her!"

"Yah!"

Adriana was thrown aside as the gunman screamed and the weapon dropped. In one smooth motion, Val picked him up and raised him over his head, taking him to the door to fling him across the deck and overboard. An incredible show of strength.

Adriana heard the splash, then a combination of yelling and running footsteps as more men abandoned the boat. But she didn't have time to count their number, since Zeke had picked up the fallen automatic. Val stood between him and the door.

"Get out of my way, you monster!" Zeke shouted.

Val's eyes seemed to glow and he showed his teeth.

Which looked pretty pointed to Adriana. If she weren't so upset, she would have cowered. If Val weren't fighting for Jennifer, for her.

Where was Jennifer, anyway? she wondered, even in the melee. Shouting her own desperation, she jumped on Zeke, trying to knock the gun away. He shoved her aside easily, pulling the trigger just as Val lunged for him. A blossom of red bloomed on Val's chest, spreading from the hole in his coat.

"Val!" Adriana screamed, fearing he'd been killed. "No!"

But her lover didn't so much as pause, toppling Zeke and lifting him by the throat. "Vermin! I should kill you!"

Instead, with tremendous force, he hurled the man against one of the boat's large portholes. Glass shattered, and Zeke lolled back unconscious, the top part of his body outside the boat, the rest inside.

Fear still held Adriana prisoner. She expected to see Val drop at any moment. But he remained standing and pushed her behind him...because Rakosi had risen from the floor. The big man fingered the medallion hanging about his neck on a chain—a pendant about the size of silver dollar—and stuck it inside his shirt.

"So, cousin, it is to be just you and I." Rakosi's eyes glittered as he stooped to pick up a large sliver of glass. In the other hand, he carried a sharpened stake. "Now you shall die, perish...as you should have long, long ago."

"It will take more than you and your flimsy weapons," said Val. "You cannot kill me while I sleep, like you did Yelena."

"Your succubus of a sister deserved what she got. I wish I had killed all of you."

"You dare to call names, lowly thief, sniveling coward?" Val lifted his chin proudly. "You feared facing any of us. You wished only to sneak inside our home and steal the medallion."

Rakosi flushed. "It was little enough legacy. It gives me powers I should have had in the first place. I am a Kadar!"

"Half a Kadar," said Val. "The Kadars are *my* family, not yours. You have affronted us." He indicated Adriana. "And now you have affronted my woman's family, as well. Where is her sister?"

"In a locker. Alive . . . at least for the moment."

A locker? Adriana glanced about.

While Val urged, "Let both of them go. They have nothing to do with you and me."

"Oh?" Rakosi hefted the stake like a spear. "I shall enjoy watching your harlot's face as you die. Then I will kill her and her sister, too. Maybe I will drain their blood like I did the other fools—"

Even as Rakosi spoke, he was lunging swiftly, striking out with his weapons. Val feinted, came back at him, but caught a jab in one hand from the shard of glass. A line of red sliced through his glove and skin, dripping blood. He cursed in Hungarian.

And Adriana cried out, already wondering how he'd survived the bullet wound. Val looked paler than normal and his breathing sounded labored. Instinctively protective, she picked up a piece of broken chair to whack Rakosi on the head.

The blow didn't faze him. He growled, turning toward her. Giving Val the chance to attack the man from the other direction. He brought Rakosi down with a huge thud and they rolled across the floor.

Adriana jumped out of the way, searching for another weapon. She picked up a piece of glass.

Rakosi had dropped his shard, but managed to jab at Val with the stake. "I will put this through your cold, black heart!"

"You are not so strong, even with the medallion!"

The medallion? It seemed to be very important. And Rakosi, whoever he was, seemed an equal match for Val. Throwing his antagonist off, Rakosi scrambled to his feet.

"The sun will be at its zenith in moments," the big man told Val, the medallion swinging against his chest as he crouched. In the fight, it had worked itself out of his shirt. "You are losing strength by the minute. I can tell."

Val did look weaker. Fearing for him and for Jennifer, Adriana made an instant, daring decision.

The medallion.

Dropping the glass, she took a running leap and landed smack on Rakosi's broad back. He grabbed for her, but she was too fast, biting down hard on his ear.

"Ya-r-rgh!"

Even as he screeched, she grabbed the medallion's chain, threw herself backward, dragging the pendant over his head.

"Ra-r-rgh!"

Rakosi's eyes were desperate as a wild animal's as he came after her, sharpened stake in hand. Val lunged at the same time, knocking him to the floor.

Rakosi screamed again but didn't rise and, to her horror, Adriana saw why. The man's fall had rammed the stake he'd been carrying into his own chest. Red seeped in a widening stain across the back of his shirt.

"He is dying," said Val, taking the medallion from Adriana's trembling fingers, then embracing her. "My lovely, brave one. Let us now find your sister."

There were several lockers in the cabin, which Val ripped open. Finding only equipment or supplies, they headed down a stairway that led below. A mirror hanging on the stairwell's wall glimmered, even when Val passed.

Because he couldn't be seen in it?

But Adriana couldn't worry about anything but finding her sister. She wasn't certain of the place they'd entered, the light being so dim. But she could hear a pounding sound.

"She is there," said Val.

He quickly located the locker where Jennifer had been deposited. Her hands tied, her mouth gagged, she'd been kicking the door with her sturdy running shoes. Val tore off the gag and lifted her in his arms.

"A-Adriana!" Jennifer gasped. "What happened? All the noise!"

"There was a terrible fight," said Adriana, touching her sister's face lovingly.

Val carried Jennifer up the stairs. Emerging into light again, he put her down and removed her bonds. She leaned against Adriana weakly, then gazed about, her eyes widening at the mess in the upstairs cabin, at Zeke hanging unconscious out the porthole, at Rakosi's body lying on the floor.

"He fell on his own weapon," Adriana told her sister.

"We have to call the police!"

"There is no time," said Val, clutching his coat about him, putting the hat back on. "I must return to my house. I am deathly ill."

CHAPTER FOURTEEN

"Ill isn't the word for a person who's been shot and sliced with glass," Adriana said as they headed back for Uptown in another taxi. Worried out of her mind, she cradled Val against her.

"Shot?" Jennifer sat by the other window. "We have to take him to a hospital."

"No hospital," stated Val, his voice sounding stronger than his physical appearance. "The bullet merely went through my shoulder. It is my allergy to the sun that has weakened me. I need rest."

"But a hospital will be better," objected Jennifer. "And we can make a police report there."

"No hospital!" rasped Val, stirring, obviously bothered. "And if you wish to speak to the police, you must contact them yourself."

Frowning, Jennifer looked as if she was about to protest again until Adriana told her, "He saved your life. Let him do what he wants."

Val added, "I am happy your sister lives, Adriana. I only wish I could have stopped Rakosi from murdering Yelena."

"Yelena?"

"His sister," explained Adriana.

Jennifer's expression softened. "That horrible man. When did that happen?"

Val sighed. "A long time ago."

"Well, he stepped up his activities in Chicago," said Jennifer. "He murdered three people in the past couple of weeks." She gazed at Adriana. "When I heard about Stone Drake, I was afraid to come home last night, decided to stay at Todd's parents' house in the suburbs. I tried to call you at the club, but I guess you didn't get my message."

Adriana shook her head. "You must have spoken to one of the bartenders. They never write down anything." Especially on a busy Saturday night. "But the morning wasn't safe, either. Rakosi must have been waiting around."

"His men were waiting," corrected Jennifer. "They broke through the back door before I knew what was going on and hauled me off to the boat. Rakosi was furious when he realized they'd brought me instead of you."

"I'm sorry." Adriana still felt guilty.

"We would have both been involved one way or the other," Jennifer insisted. She shivered. "Before he threw me into the locker, Rakosi bragged about the murders and threatened me with the equipment he'd used—plastic tubing with sharp metal fittings for stabbing into the jugular. And a big bottle for the blood. Ugh!"

"Poor Jens," murmured Adriana.

"Poor him," said Jennifer, gazing at Val.

With alarm, Adriana noted how sharp his cheekbones suddenly appeared, how shadowy the hollows beneath his eyes. He lay so still against her. In his weakened state, she supposed they could force him to go to a hospital. But, instinctively, she felt that it wouldn't be right to cross his wishes.

When the taxi let them out in Uptown, however, she insisted on staying with him, while Jennifer returned home.

"Don't even bother protesting," she said as he leaned against her to climb the steps of the Victorian mansion. "I'm going to put you to bed and take care of you."

"You do not know what you do. You do not know what I am."

What he was. Adriana didn't want to think about what she'd witnessed. Everything had happened so fast, she hoped she'd been under some sort of delusion. But as far as superhuman strength was concerned, she knew that Rakosi had been pretty much equal to Val. And he certainly hadn't been a vampire if he'd needed equipment to get blood out of people.

When she finally put Val to bed and helped him out of his coat and jacket, he broke into a sweat, starting to rave, "My sword . . . iron . . . bloodstones." He tried to sit up. "The enemy is at the gates!"

Enemies? Swords? She brought a candle to the bed, soothing him, "No, no. Don't worry, we're safe. Everything is okay."

He fell back, tossing his head so restlessly she tried to plump his pillow. It seemed hard and a few grains of earth sifted out onto the sheet. A pillow stuffed with dirt?

Adriana told herself that the dog must have been on the bed with dirty paws.

"My family," Val gasped. "For them, I melted the sword . . . and forged the medallion—"

The medallion.

Adriana wondered if he'd feel better with his hard-won treasure in hand. She fetched the heavy pendant from his coat pocket, noting it did seem to be made of iron and was set with brownish red gems that could very well be bloodstones.

"Ah-h!" He clutched the medallion, immediately calming as he pressed it against his heart.

She knelt beside the bed and unbuttoned his shirt to examine the bullet wound. It looked smaller than she expected and wasn't bleeding profusely. But at the least, "You need antibiotics."

"The wound is clean. The bullet went through," he said, sounding more lucid. "It was the sun—"

"Sunlight can make you this sick?"

"So sick I may perish."

Her heart nearly stopped. She hadn't known he was that ill! "You might die? My God, we've got to take you to a hospital!"

"No!"

Even if he weren't so adamant, she knew she couldn't carry him and he had no phone with which to call an ambulance. She started to cry.

"Please do not weep."

"I'll go out to the street and try to find another taxi!"

"There is no time. Listen to me, Adriana." He pulled her closer. "A key lies in an envelope in that top dresser drawer. It and the password written on the outside will allow you access to my bank box. Remove the money. A large amount. Keep it for yourself."

"I don't want to think about money."

"Money is the least I can offer you." He took hold of her hand. "But send the medallion to my family. Do you have a piece of paper? I will give you their address."

She rose to find her purse and the little notebook and pen she always carried. Her hand trembling, she felt a chill when she wrote down what he dictated. "Kisvarka, Hungary."

Home of The Kadar.

Her attention returned to Val when he started shivering.

"My sword!" he cried.

"What about your sword?"

"Only iron from my own hand... shall harness the cravings of my family. Watch out for Rakosi!"

He was raving again. She offered comfort. "Rakosi's gone."

He paid no attention, babbling on, "He stole it from Yelena... stabbed her through the heart. Foul *dhampir!*"

"Damper?"

"Dhampir." His pronunciation was different, making the word rhyme with vampire. "Rakosi... the son of my uncle and a village woman. Powerful... but angry and jealous. And not a Kadar, not even with the medallion—"

Then he jerked, eyes rolling.

"Val!"

He shuddered, didn't seem aware that she clutched his chilly hand in hers. "I owe my family. May God hear me! I led them into wrongdoing... to save our people."

Then he lapsed into heavy-breathing silence, scaring her even more. She thought about running out to the street again and started to rise, only to have him jerk her down.

"You!"

Scared, she stared into dull brown eyes that held only a hint of fiery gold. Compassion replaced her fear. "What do you want, Val? Just tell me."

"I have found what I have always wanted—you." He seemed lucid again. "You are my soul mate, Adriana."

Her throat constricted. "I love you, too."

"If only we had met . . . sooner."

She couldn't stand it! "You're not going to die!" she cried. "I won't let you!"

"You cannot argue with God or the devil."

"I can damned well try!"

And she kissed the hand she held, rubbed it against her face. Tasting something salty, coppery, she licked her lips, then kissed his hand again, finally realizing it was the one with the open wound.

"What do you do?" Val demanded, visibly upset. "You have taken my blood, Adriana! Now the choice is taken from you."

Meaning she was a vampire, too? Because everything they'd been talking about fit the stupid legend Irina had told her about. Legends meant nothing, though, when compared to life and death . . . or love. She still wasn't certain what she'd seen or heard, and she didn't care.

Valentin Kadar lay dying, and she mourned him with her heart and soul.

He was losing consciousness, his eyes closing, his breathing slowing. His skin seemed waxy. She felt for a pulse, so faint it barely existed. "Val?"

He didn't respond. Couldn't. She was certain he now lay in a coma.

Weeping even harder, she eased herself into the bed beside him. "I love you no matter who or what you are, Val."

For if, by some slim chance, he really was The Kadar, he'd done what he had to save his countrymen. He valued loyalty and loved his family, coming to America to retrieve the medallion that seemed so important to them. Rakosi had been the real monster, the murderer who'd struck down Val's sister and Eddie and Lilly and Stone... plus who knew how many more.

While Val had fought for life, giving his own to save *her* sister. He couldn't be evil, not in her book.

Thinking of all they'd shared, of the deep passion she still felt for him, she slid an arm across his chest, placing her hand on the medallion that lay over his heart.

With little surprise, she realized he now had no pulse at all. His skin felt cold, his limbs rigid.

Valentin Kadar was dead.

And Adriana closed her eyes, not caring if she died, as well.

Someone approaches.

Adriana awoke and rose to her elbows, gazing through the darkness of the room. Listening carefully, she heard the scrape of footsteps on the sidewalk outside. From the weight of the footfall, the heaviness of the visitor's breathing, she knew it was a man.

Val lay beside her and she reached for him...realizing once again why he was so still.

Her throat clenched.

The least she could do was stop anyone from harming his body.

Slipping out of bed, she glided quickly, silently, to the bedroom door, entered the hallway and descended the stairs. Her movements light, flowing, she found herself at the entrance as the visitor mounted the porch. She opened the door before he even knocked.

Surprise on his face, along with something else—fear?—he stepped back. "Good evening, Ms. Thorn."

"Detective Panchella. I should have known you'd be visiting."

"Uh, I have a question or two."

"I'm sure. But did you check out the boat on the river over near Clybourn? Did you talk to my sister?"

"Yeah, yeah." He made a dismissive gesture. "Kadar's in the clear. The motorist who called in the last murder gave a description that fit Miklos Rakosi. And then there was Jennifer's statement and the equipment we found on the *Buckthorn.*" He added, "Hell of a battle musta took place there."

"Quite fierce. But Val felt he had to save my sister."

"Uh-huh." Panchella continued giving her the eye, as if she looked strange or threatening or something.

She smoothed her hair.

"You okay?" He glanced behind her. "Kadar all right?"

"He's fine," she said, figuring it wasn't any of Panchella's business. "But he's resting at the moment. I don't want to disturb him."

"Don't need to. This is an unofficial visit." He paused. "Just wanted to ask about the two of you. And—"

"And?"

He stepped back as if her glance were a baleful glare. Was her makeup smeared?

"Some of those guys that were working for Rakosi said some real weird things. Seemed to think Kadar has fangs and glowing eyes." He went on quickly, "But I figure they musta been blasted on something."

"I'm sure."

He glanced at her again, then made as if to go. "Guess that's it, then." He gestured. "Still no lights in the damned house. How can you see?"

No lights?

She hadn't even noticed. Adriana led Panchella out. As she closed the door, she glanced about. Each and every piece of furniture was clearly visible, every crack in the woodwork, every tear in the aged wallpaper. The dim light of the streetlights through a few windows was more than enough. Her eyesight was better than it had ever been in her life.

Her hearing also seemed amplified, she realized, catching the sound of something moving on the stairs. One of the animals?

No...she sensed a human-size presence....

Turning, heart in her throat, she faced a dark figure. Her jaw dropped and she froze as she realized who he was. "Val! How can this be...?"

But her words evaporated like smoke as he came toward her. Running to him, flinging herself on him, she kissed his face, his neck, his hands. "I thought you were dead!"

He kissed her back, enclosed her tightly in a embrace. "Not so dead that I cannot hear your soul crying out for me." He held her as she wept anew, with joy. "I did not know if I should return this time myself. I do not believe I would have if you had not refused to leave me, had not nestled in my arms."

When she was able to speak again, she said, "I was certain your heart had stopped."

"But it began beating again...for you. Your love restored me."

Or else he'd slipped in and out of a near-death state. She also noticed that his hand seemed to have healed as he caressed her, kissed her lips, nibbled at her throat.

"I could hardly stand the grief!" she went on, venting her feelings. "We'd found each other, then lost each other. And we were perfect together. We could have married—"

"Marriage?" he said, his voice a soft rasp. "You are proposing, Adriana?"

She touched his cheek lovingly. "Am I being too forward?"

"There is nothing you can do that I would not find wonderful. I adore you," he professed, his eyes gold again, full of fire. "I love you more than words can say. And I will marry you. I *must* marry you—it is the least I can do."

"The least you can do?" She didn't like that. But her irritation was nothing in comparison to the grief she'd felt while thinking he was dead.

He went on, sounding resigned, a little sad. "You will need my guidance, dear one. Our lives will be problematic at times, not of the ordinary sort. And the melancholy can be overwhelming."

She wasn't certain what he was getting at, but she insisted, "I have no intention of feeling sad. I can find the positive side of anything."

"Even a husband who has committed many terrible deeds?"

"They couldn't have been that terrible. You're honorable and have real integrity."

"You do not know my history—"

She placed her fingers against his lips. "And you don't have to recite it now."

She wasn't ready to know the whole truth yet. "Good deeds help balance bad ones, you know."

"It would take seven centuries to make up for what I've done."

"Three and a half—with two of us working at it."

He sighed, but he sounded more satisfied than melancholy. "You *are* the one."

She raised her brows. "The one?"

"The woman I have been searching for—my soul mate, my heart, my life."

As he was hers. She kissed him hungrily, fiercely. He called forth passionate cravings she'd never felt before. The world outside spun on its axis among the stars. Night beckoned, speaking its own language.

Though in a dialect she'd never heard clearly before.

For she had changed, reality had changed...while at the same time, she trusted that her love and her bond with Valentin Kadar would always remain the same.

Val held his wife's hand and gazed at her adoringly as they sat in the café where they often took their nightly meal. "The little Gypsy is seeking you."

"Irina?" Adriana turned toward the window, removing her dark glasses. "Right, she's coming down the street." As he already knew. Adriana's own sensitivities were growing sharper with each passing evening.

He gazed at her, again admiring her intense silvery eyes, her perfect ivory complexion, her glossy dark hair. Not that many other people noticed her. No one paid much attention to either of them unless they wanted them to.

When Irina entered the restaurant, Val stood and offered her a seat.

"What a gentleman you are," the redhead quipped, though she didn't sound quite comfortable. "From a very old school."

He tried to put her at ease as he sat down again. "You can relax, little Gypsy. You are safe. Things change."

He sprinkled herbs on his rare steak, then Adriana's. "Predators do not have to go after prey on the hoof. They can be tamed."

Irina sighed. "I'm trying to be open-minded."

Adriana assured the redhead, "I'm your friend and I always will be." She added, "Since you and some other important people didn't get to attend our wedding, we thought we'd have a reception. Around ten or so, next Monday? You'll want to see the house. I'm fixing it up. Good thing it's big, with room enough for the dog, an owl and all those bats and cats."

"Is Phantom okay?"

"She has her own suite. She likes the new environment."

"Speaking of new, I heard you're only going to be working weekends now."

Adriana nodded. "I'm doing a radio talk show on some of the weekday nights. It gives troubled people the chance to speak to someone when they're all alone out there in the dark." She went on, "I always thought I preferred working with a live audience, but I'm finding I can 'sense' caller's thoughts and feelings if I really try, even when they're miles away."

Irina quirked her brows. "I'm sure."

"You know that Val is funding a shelter, don't you?" Adriana continued. "A program for the homeless and abused. Sometimes I tell callers to go there."

"You always said you loved lost souls." Irina gazed pointedly at Val.

Who only smiled. "And she saves lost souls, too." His wife had put her plans for accomplishing good deeds into action right away.

"Nothing is lost forever," stated Adriana. "Whenever the tiniest molecule changes, it simply becomes something else. Which reminds me of the new monologue I wrote for Saturday—"

"Day to night.

"Light to darkness.

"The sun sinks below the city skyline, trailing fiery silks. The moon rises, awash with diamond stars.

"Night to day. Waking. Sleeping.

"Both are reality.

"The earth is a great I-Ching ball, a black-and-white wheel of a mandala that spins out our lives.

"Love makes the difference.

"I waited for you at the edge of the world. I called. You answered...and flew to me on the mist that rises from the lake.

"Mind and heart.

"Soul and body.

"Now we will share the night forever... my one and only love."

* * * * *